Murder on Heartbreak Trail

A Violet Hartwell Airstreams and Apparitions Mystery

D.W. MARONEY

DEDICATION

To the fearless women of Stella's Sisters.
I want to be like you when I grow up.

ACKNOWLEDGMENTS

First, and foremost, I have to thank the fabulous women who belong to Airstream® International's Stella's Sisters group for welcoming me into their fold for a few enlightening days. Many thanks to their president, Charissa Wyatt, whose life on the road sparked my muse into action.

For those who aren't familiar with the group, the Stella's Sisters are women who tow their travel trailers all by themselves. They are a group of fiercely independent women who live by their own rules and meet every challenge and fear head-on. I found them to be smart, funny, welcoming, and proud. I can't help but admire all they've accomplished and admit to a bit of jealousy regarding their travels. I wish them all the best and hope my characters do them justice.

"The woman who follows the crowd will usually go no
further than the crowd.
The woman who walks alone is likely to find
herself in places no one has ever been before."
Albert Einstein

PROLOGUE

"What are you doing out here?"

I didn't flinch at the sound of my dead husband's voice in the quiet confines of the camper. I didn't scream. Or run. Or even cry. The last few days, I'd done all that and more. Blessed numbness had set in. Going stark raving mad seemed like the logical next step. "I couldn't stand it in there another minute." I nodded out the open door, where I had a direct view into the house through the kitchen window. People milled around, all with long faces as they mourned the loss of their friend, coworker, loved one.

"How long are they going to stay?"

"I don't know. I wish they'd all leave right now." I couldn't wait to get out of the black dress I'd borrowed from my sister and into something comfortable and colorful. The only black in my closet was a LBD, Little Black Dress, I wore to cocktail parties when nothing else would be acceptable. Stylish but plain, it was easy to change the look with a new scarf or jewelry, so no one ever suspected it was the same dress I'd worn countless times, or if they did, they were nice enough not to say anything. My fashionista sister took one look at my sad offering and declared it inappropriate for a funeral. "My feet hurt."

Mason's deep chuckle pierced a hole in my heart, right next to the one his death had drilled. Nevertheless, the familiar sound made me turn to look in the direction it had come. Mason Hartwell lounged with his arms crossed and his shoulders braced against the built-in refrigerator.

Grief does crazy things to people. Hallucinations are definitely crazy. "Mason?"

"Don't look so shocked, Vi. You didn't think I'd leave you all alone, did you?"

"I…" I closed my eyes and inhaled deeply before forcing the air out of my lungs the way the grief counselor the bureau had sent over had taught me. When I opened my eyes again, the apparition was still there, an indulgent smile on his handsome face.

"I don't understand it either, Vi. I'm just as shocked as you are to be standing here unalive, but I've decided not to question it. Every extra minute I get to spend with you is a blessing, even if I can't touch you."

I glanced at the kitchen window. No one had noticed I'd left; if they had, they were giving me space. Ignoring the way my new shoes, again, compliments of my well-meaning sister, pinched my feet, I stood and faced the vision. "How do you know you can't touch me?"

Mason straightened to his full height, a good six inches over my five-foot-six. "Because I tried. At the funeral."

I touched my shoulder.

"You felt that?"

"It was a breeze, a draft in the church."

"It was me. I wanted you to know I was there."

Anger bubbled to the surface. The man, ghost, or whatever he was, had a lot of explaining to do. If I were on the path to madness, I might as well go all the way, full steam ahead. "Why?"

"I hated seeing you look so broken."

I shook my head. "No. Not why did you touch me? Why did you leave me? What happened?" All I'd gotten from the police was that his car had veered off the road into a steep canyon. "You're too good a driver to have taken a curve like that too fast. One you've taken hundreds of times."

"I don't know, Violet." His face screwed up in confusion. "I wasn't going too fast. I know that. One minute, I was thinking about how much fun we were going to have on our camping adventure, and the next, I was going over the edge. That's all I remember. I'm sorry. This isn't what you signed up for."

"I vowed for better or for worse, and this is the very worst, Mason." Blinking back tears I didn't think I had in me, I cocked my head toward the house. "I don't think I can go back in there knowing you aren't coming back."

"Then don't."

"What do you mean? I have to. It's our home."

Mason's shrug and devilish grin were so familiar, I had to fight back more tears. I was going to miss that side of him. There was no room for levity in his job with the FBI, but at home, he loved to joke around. "The camper is ready to go. So, go. The house and the memories will all be there when you get back."

"I can't just leave."

"Sure, you can. I hitched the truck and trailer the night before…"

"Before you drove off the road?" I didn't know what was worse, the anger I harbored for my dead husband or the fact that I was talking to him as if he were really there.

"I'd change that if I could, Vi. You know I would." His steady gaze held a world of understanding and regret. "Take the camper, Violet. Go see the country, like we planned. You can always come back home, but if you stay, you might never find the courage to leave."

He was right about that. Every step outside the house, except the ones that had brought me to the camper, had been fraught with fear and uncertainty. Somehow, the camper had seemed safe. My thoughts, as always, went to our twins. "What about M.J. and Elle? They're heartbroken. What will they think if I just drive away?"

"They're adults with significant others to lean on. Call them from the road and tell them what you told me—that you need to get away from the memories for a while. They'll understand."

"What if they don't?"

"You've lived your life for them, and for me, and no one appreciates that more than I do, but it's time to live your life for yourself. You need to find out who you are without me and the kids to take care of."

"And I'm supposed to do that in a camper?"

"Yes."

"You make it sound so simple."

"It is, Vi." He gave me an appraising look. "Black is not your color, sweetheart. Change into something comfortable. The spare key to the truck is in the drawer next to the flatware."

I glanced over my shoulder at the drawer next to the sink. Could I? Mason made it sound so easy. Just hop in the truck and go. Where? His untimely demise meant they'd missed the first campground reservation on their itinerary. "If I left tonight…" I gasped. Mason was gone. Really gone.

I'm losing my mind. Talking to a ghost. Another peek through the kitchen window made my stomach twist with anxiety. *I can't go back in there. Not yet.* Reaching over, I slid the flatware drawer open, and like the apparition or my subconscious had said, the spare key to the truck lay inside next to a wallet containing some cash, and several credit cards we'd earmarked for gas and expenses along the way, and a copy of my driver's license. The key was warm in my hand, and it felt more right than I thought it should, as the idea of leaving solidified in my mind. Healing was out there somewhere. I just had to find it.

CHAPTER ONE

"I'm glad that's over." My shoulders dropped, and my knuckles regained their normal color as I released my grip on the steering wheel. "Does this get any easier?"

"You did great, Vi. Next time, you won't even need my help."

"That's what you think." I waved back at the woman from the next campsite who had watched me back the monstrous travel trailer into its home for the next few weeks. "Couldn't you have bought something smaller?"

Not receiving an answer, I glanced at the empty passenger seat, where an apparition of my late husband had sat seconds before. And before that, he'd stood outside, waving his arms and using hand signals to help me negotiate the tight parking space. In the weeks since I'd driven away from his wake without a word to anyone, he'd popped up during my most stressful times to provide support and words of encouragement. I'd gotten better at parking the Airstream trailer, but the thought of backing it into a tree raised my blood pressure, and more than once, it had brought tears to my eyes as the enormity of doing everything on my own overwhelmed me.

Pasting a smile on my face, I cut the engine on the heavy-duty truck needed to tow the trailer and popped the door open. I stepped down to the pine-needle-coated ground. All that was left to do was unhook the trailer from the truck, level it, and hook it up to the utilities. Then I could break out the bottle of wine I'd picked up from a winery I visited the day before.

Bent over the trailer hitch, I almost jumped out of my skin at the sound of a disembodied voice—not my dear Mason's. This one had a decidedly Southern accent and sounded female. "Hey there. Welcome!" A pair of dusty feet clad in Birkenstocks came into sight. I blew a stray lock of hair out of my face and straightened to greet my temporary neighbor. "That was some mighty fine parking. Maybe you could teach me how to do that? It takes me half a dozen tries to get my rig in straight. I'm Bernice." She stuck a weathered and not-so-clean hand out to shake. "Everyone calls me Bea. What's your name?"

I wiped my hand on my shorts, then shook Bea's hand. "Violet. Everybody calls me Violet."

"Well, welcome to Singing Pines, Violet. How long are you fixin' to stay?"

"My reservation is for a month, but I don't know." I shrugged, a habit I'd picked up from Mason but had only recently noticed. "I'm not sure I'll stay that long."

"You got someplace else to be?"

I shook my head. "No." I still couldn't see myself living alone in the house I'd shared with Mason for almost thirty years. Recently, I'd thought about signing it over to my adult kids, but what would I do then? Living in a trailer and constantly moving around didn't sound appealing either.

"That's what I thought. Every campground this side of the Mississippi is booked solid until after Labor Day. If you've got a space guaranteed until then, best you stay there."

"There must be something. Somewhere."

Bea's laughter rang through the dense forest surrounding the campground. A few birds took flight. Judging by the lines carved deep into her sun-weathered face, the woman was sixty if she was a day. Despite it being summer, she wore a long-sleeved shirt and baggy jeans. A long gray ponytail peeked out of a floppy straw hat that had seen better days.

"What's so funny?"

"Never would have pegged you as a newbie!" She slapped both hands on her thighs. "You parked your rig like a pro, but if you think you're going to find a new place to camp before the summer tourists go home, you're as green as a toad frog."

I drank in the compliment on my parking like it was holy water, even as I cringed at being compared to a frog. *I might be green, but I'm learning. I can do this.* "This is my third campground. I only stayed a week in the first one and two in the second one."

"What was wrong with them?"

"Too many families." I love kids, but the happy families were an unwelcome reminder of all I'd lost.

"Well, Violet, you've come to the right campground. Everyone on this side of the park travels solo. The noisy kids are all on the side with the pool and playground. All the Hitchin' the Road Ladies are over here."

"Hitchin' the Road Ladies?"

"It's a club I belong to. All single women who tow their own trailers. Not everyone here is a member, but most are. We travel in packs. There are hundreds of club members scattered throughout the country. Some live in their trailers. Others are seasonal campers. There are five of us at this campground right now. We're getting together at my trailer tonight. You should come. Everyone brings something to share, but since it's your first time, just bring yourself, a chair, and a bottle of wine, if you have one to spare. If not, just bring an empty glass or cup, or whatever you have."

"That's really…"

"Don't say nice. Not until you've met everybody. Cocktails are at five. Don't be late.

CHAPTER TWO

"You should go, Vi."

I blew out a breath as I stepped out of the shower to find I wasn't alone. Clutching a towel around me, I let Mason see my frustration. "Where were you when I was fighting with the trailer hitch and couldn't get the water line connected?"

"You didn't need my help, but I was there. Bea seems nice, and you could use some friends on the road."

The idea of making friends gave a permanence to my wandering that I wasn't ready for. I still wasn't ready to face my old life back home, but I hadn't fully committed to this one either. "I don't need friends. I've got you." I pulled on a pair of turquoise Capri-length yoga pants covered with splotches of neon purple. I topped the outfit with a purple sports bra and a matching T-shirt.

"Neither of us knows how long I'll be here, Vi. I could be gone tomorrow for all I know."

"Please don't say that, Mason." Perched on the edge of the built-in bed, I donned my socks and walking shoes. Practiced moves had my shoulder-length hair in a high ponytail.

"It's true, and you know it. I'd leave right now if I could. My being here is keeping you from dealing with your grief and moving forward with your new life."

Our conversation was getting tedious. I grabbed a water bottle from the refrigerator. "Going on the road by myself isn't moving forward?"

"No. Not if you refuse to meet new people."

"They'll ask questions I'm not ready to answer."

"You're going to have to talk about it eventually, sweetheart. That's part of the grieving process."

I narrowed my eyes at the apparition. "You want me to go over there and tell a bunch of strangers that I'm mad as hell at my husband for driving off the road and leaving me to face the rest of my life alone? Is that what you want me to do? Has it occurred to you that I'm avoiding people because I can't talk about you without wanting to throw something?"

"Then throw something, Vi, scream and shout, and throw a tantrum. Maybe if you do, I can go."

A hysterical laugh bubbled up. Was he for real? "What?"

Mason shrugged. "It's just a thought. Maybe your grief is what's holding me here."

"Oh no, you don't! You are *not* placing blame on my shoulders. I don't know why you're here, but I know it's not my fault. *I* didn't drive your car off the road. You did that all by yourself, Mason Hartwell." I was well and truly furious now. "You took that curve too fast and lost control. I don't know why or how, but none of that was my fault, so if you think it's my grief that's keeping you here, you can be on your way. I don't need you!"

The door made a satisfying sound when I slammed it on my way out. Mason could make a saint swear with his know-it-all attitude. We'd disagreed many times in the twenty-nine years we'd been married, but I'd never been as angry with him as I had been since he'd driven off that road. Now, I couldn't seem to shake the anger. It kept me awake at night and fueled the nervous energy that kept me going day after day when all I wanted to do was curl up in my mobile bunk and die.

Blinded by tears, I struck out along the road leading to the campground's main entrance. If I recalled correctly, several hiking trails either crossed or began close to my campsite. A brisk walk would allow me to work off some of my anger. If I could get my emotions under control, maybe I'd join Bea and the others for dinner, or at least an after-dinner drink. Mason was right about one thing. If I were going to do this camping thing for a long time, it would be good to make some friends along the way. Spending three weeks in the same spot and not speaking to anyone might make me crazier than I already am. I'd already spent three weeks in isolation if you didn't count conversations with a ghost.

He might be right about making friends, but he was dead

wrong about my grief being the reason he hadn't moved on to wherever souls go. I'd grieved the loss of loved ones before, and none of them had ever hung around to give me unsolicited advice. None had even seen fit to answer me when I'd called upon them for guidance. Whatever Mason's reason for staying was, it had nothing to do with my grief.

"He'd best look at his own problems for answers," I mumbled as I trudged up a steep grade lined with tall pines.

"Don't you think I've done that, Vi?"

I stumbled, my foot slipping off the worn path. Reaching out, I caught a low-hanging branch to arrest my fall down the steep embankment. "Shit, Mason. You have to quit sneaking up on me."

"Sorry. I didn't mean to scare you, and I didn't mean to blame you for…whatever this is." He gestured to his ethereal self, then, seeing my predicament, asked, "You need some help?"

"What are you going to do? Call 9-1-1?" We'd long since figured out Mason's help was limited to advice. Offering a hand to help me back onto the trail wouldn't do any good. I was on my own.

"Not funny, Vi. Get yourself back up here. Fast."

"What do you think I'm trying to do?" I bent at the waist, grabbed another branch, and working hand-over-hand, inched my way closer to the trail. "Last thing I need is the kids getting a phone call telling them their mother died sliding down a canyon." Yes, it was a low blow, but I wasn't done being mad at Mason yet. He hadn't been there when I'd had to tell Elle and M.J. what had happened. The horror of it would remain with me for the rest of my life.

Feet planted on firm ground again, I brushed a lock of hair out of my eyes with the back of my hand. "Violet. Listen to me." Mason reserved his FBI Special Agent voice for work. Hearing it in the middle of the forest made the hair on the back of my neck stand on end. "I need you to find some rocks, flat ones you can stack, and make a little tower right there." He pointed to the spot where I'd slipped off the trail. "Then I want you to go back the way you came. When you get in cellphone range, call 9-1-1 and tell the dispatcher there's a dead body about half a mile up on Heartbreak Trail, near the overlook. Tell them you'll meet them at the trailhead inside the campground."

"What are you talking about? There isn't a body here."

"Yes, there is. You almost fell right on top of it."

I shook my head. "No. No, I didn't. That's not poss…possible."

"Trust me, Vi. There's a dead body down there. I've seen enough of them to know."

"Maybe it's just a pile of clothes?"

A chill brushed my shoulders as Mason reached out to me. Bending so he was on eye level with me, he shook his head. "Stack the rocks to mark the spot. Then you need to go, Violet. He hasn't been dead long. The sooner a forensic team gets here, the better."

I didn't dare look down the hillside as I heaped rocks into a pile I could recognize later on. Wiping my hands on my leggings, I glanced around, committing the area to memory. "They're going to ask me what I saw." I hadn't been married to a law enforcement officer for most of my life without learning a thing or two about procedure. "I can't tell them a ghost told me about the body. They'll lock me up first and ask questions later."

"Tell them the truth: you got too close to the edge of the trail, and your foot slipped. When you stopped yourself, you saw the man's boots and his trousers. Then you noticed the flies, and that's when you knew he was dead."

I wrapped my arms tight around my stomach. "I'm going to be sick."

"No, you're not. You're stronger than that, Vi. Go. I'll be with you the whole time."

"Promise?"

"Promise."

CHAPTER THREE

"Is it true?"

At the sound of my neighbor's voice, I jerked my head up.
Dark had fallen over the campground in the hours since I'd
reported the body on the trail. There was plenty of daylight left
when I started out, and I hadn't planned to be gone long enough to
need a flashlight. I should have taken the officer up on his offer to
drive me back to my rig, but I'd had enough of their questions and
disbelieving looks to last a lifetime. Despite there being a killer on
the loose, I'd felt safe enough with Mason watching over me until
Bea's voice scared the bejeezus out of me. Hand on my chest to
still my runaway heart, I faced the older woman. "Is what true?"

"Did you find Ned dead up on Heartbreak Trail?"

"Uhm." I opened my door, reached in, and flicked a switch.
The string of patio lights I'd hung along the edge of my awning
provided ambiance more than illumination, but I felt better. Safer.
Closing my door, I wrapped my arms around my middle and faced
my inquisitive neighbor. Only now, there were five of them. All
ages. All shapes and sizes. All staring at me. "Yes. I found a body
while I was out for a walk. The police said it was Ned—the guy
who owns the campground?"

"What else did they say?"

I searched the group for the one who had asked the question.
A woman not much older than my daughter raised her hand.
"We've been dying to know what happened to him."

"Shush, Millie!" Bea scolded. "Have some respect for the
dead." My gaze met hers. "You've had a rough go of it today,
haven't you? Well, come on over. I bet you haven't had anything

to eat, have you?"

"No." The women parted like well-oiled saloon doors, letting Bea and me through before closing ranks behind us. A few short steps later, I sat in a camp chair in front of the portable fire pit. In moments, a plate piled high with a hamburger and several types of salads appeared in my hands. There had to be a million calories on the heavy paper plate, but I didn't have it in my mind to care. Once the shock had worn off, I was ravenous.

"Kendra, get her something to drink. Willa, fetch the throw from my easy chair." Bea issued orders like a drill sergeant. As things materialized around me, I got the impression these women were used to following Bea's orders. "Eat." Bea gestured to the full plate sitting on my lap. "When you're done, we want to hear all about it."

Who was I to argue with the Queen Bea? Smiling at my new name for my neighbor, I ate until I couldn't stuff another bite in my mouth. The moment I set the plate aside, the inquisition began.

"Was he dead when you found him?"

"Was there a lot of blood?"

"Was he murdered?"

"Did you see anyone else on the trail?"

"Did he slip and fall to his death? That trail is dangerous." This from a stout woman named Sherry, who took credit for the Hominy Salad I had scarfed down like it was ambrosia. She seemed the type to know a dangerous trail when she saw one.

Bea refilled my plastic cup, aka wine glass. "Take your time, Violet. We aren't going anywhere."

I took a few sips while I thought about how to answer the women's questions. They were a curious bunch, but I guessed there wasn't much excitement in a life on the road. A murder in their small community of travelers would stir interest. And it had been murder. No doubt about that. Ned had been stabbed multiple times, ruling out suicide or accidentally falling on his own knife. The fact that no weapon had been found sort of sealed the deal. The local police had a homicide on their hands, and the first place they would look would be the person who found the body.

Placing my cup on the folding camp table next to my chair, I pulled Bea's throw tighter around my shoulders. "I don't know much," I began. "I went for a walk, and I must have gotten too close to the edge of the trail, and the next thing I knew, my foot slipped. I slid down the slope until my foot hit something solid. I thought it was a rock." A chorus of gasps rose from my audience.

"Oh. My. God." Willa folded both hands over my heart. "You could have been killed!"

"I wasn't, though."

"You need some hiking boots. Those trainers you've got on aren't gonna cut it on the trails." This, from Stout Sherry, who obviously knew a thing or two about hiking. It wasn't a bad suggestion. I made a mental note to go into town soon for more suitable footwear.

Kendra scooted to the edge of her chair. "What did you do?"

I repeated the story that Mason and I concocted on our way down to call 9-1-1. "I used some low-hanging branches to pull myself back up to the trail." That much was true. "It wasn't until I was safe on the trail again that I looked down the slope and realized a man's boot had stopped me from sliding to the bottom of the hill. It took me a few moments to realize the boot was attached to a body." It was Mason who first noticed the boot that prevented me from sliding to the bottom of the ravine. Most of what I knew firsthand came from watching the detectives examine the remains later on.

"Yikes! That must have been terrifying."

Despite the fire and the warm blanket, a shiver raced down my spine.

Kendra leaned forward. "Did you know it was Ned when you saw the body?"

I shook my head. "No. I'd only seen him once, and that was such a brief encounter. His wife was behind the desk when I checked in. Ned only came out of the back office once while I was there to answer a question from one of the other campers."

"Like I said," Sherry interjected. "That trail is dangerous. They need to put a railing up so accidents like this one don't happen."

"It wasn't an accident."

"What?" They all questioned at once.

"Ned was murdered."

CHAPTER FOUR

My audience stared at me in silence as they processed my statement. I glanced across the way at my temporary home. Mason leaned against the bright aluminum trailer, his arms and ankles crossed in a casual pose I knew well. He smiled indulgently at me, a silent endorsement of my socializing. His approval felt good, but what I wouldn't give to feel his arms around me again. He'd always made me feel safe. With a killer on the loose, I needed his warmth and strength more than ever.

Queen Bea's voice snapped my attention back to my audience. "Are you sure?"

I nodded. "He was stabbed to death. And whoever did it took the knife with them." They were still combing the surrounding area for the murder weapon when I left, so it seemed reasonable to me that the culprit had taken it with him. Or her.

"Oh, my!" Willa swooned but recovered after a fortifying sip of wine.

Kendra refilled Willa's paper cup, then tipped some of the dark liquid into my cup. "Do the police have any idea who did it?"

I paused, letting the question hang there for a moment. "I got the impression that I'm their prime suspect."

"What?" They sounded like a chorus of screech owls as they all spoke at once.

"That's just plain nonsense," Queen Bea declared. "You said yourself you didn't know the man. Why in the world would they think you murdered him?"

"I reported the body on the trail, and since Ned hadn't been dead all that long, I can't blame them for putting me at the top of their suspect list. I'm certain they'll find the real killer soon, and I'll be free to go about my business."

"You're not free now?"

I shrugged. "They asked me not to leave town until I'm cleared. Come tomorrow, I bet they have someone in custody."

***

An early morning knock on my door woke me from a fitful sleep. My newfound friends assured me that everything was going to be okay, but I wasn't so sure. There was a killer out there somewhere, and they didn't want to be found. Wiping sleep from my eyes, I swung my feet to the floor. "Put a robe and shoes on, Vi."

I glanced at my husband's apparition. He'd always been a good-looking man, but this version of him never had a hair out of place or wrinkled clothing, while I still resembled a vagabond first thing in the morning. It really wasn't fair. "Why?" I yawned as I slid my toes into the flip-flops next to the bed. "Who's out there?"

"The local cops. They're here to search the truck and trailer."

His words were like a shot of caffeine, bringing me instantly awake. "Don't they have something better to do?"

"Apparently not."

A heavy fist pounded the door.

"Violet Hartwell! We've got a warrant! Open up!"

"Cooperate, but don't say anything, Violet. Not one blessed word. Do you hear me?"

"I hear you."

"And take your purse with you!"

I gave the apparition a mock salute as I made my way to the door.

Three uniformed officers and one in plain clothes, a detective, I guessed, pushed their way inside the moment I opened the door. It was the detective who followed me outside after obtaining the keys to my super-duty pickup.

"What's going on?" Queen Bea joined me beneath the awning. I handed the older woman the document I'd been given.

"A search warrant? For what? You didn't do anything."

"You and I know that, but they haven't gotten the message yet." I eyed the steam rising from Bea's coffee mug. "Got any more of that? My eyes are open, but I'm not firing on all cylinders yet."

"Have a seat. I'll be right back."

I sat in the only camp chair I'd bothered to unpack and casually placed my purse behind my feet. My bathrobe pooled on the ground, hiding the item from view. Even though the victim had been stabbed, I didn't know the legalities of carrying a gun in my purse in this state, and I wasn't in a hurry to find out either. For the first time since Mason had insisted I get my concealed carry permit, I wished I hadn't done it.

"I didn't know how you took your coffee." Bea handed me a steaming mug, then slung a folded camp chair off her shoulder and flicked it open. "Figured something like this called for strong and black anyway."

"You got that right." I inhaled, savoring the heavenly smell. I offered my neighbor a weak smile. "Thank you."

"No problem. Us single women have to stick together. We're targets for all kinds of craziness. Take this search, for example." She nodded toward my rig. "If you had a man traveling with you, they wouldn't look twice at you, but being alone, and Ned being the kind of man he was, they automatically assume the worst about you."

I took a tentative sip of the fragrant brew. Judging it cool enough to drink, I brought the mug to my lips again. "What kind of man was Ned?"

"Skirt chaser. Womanizer." Bea's shrug reminded me of Mason. "They all apply. You might be the only woman he didn't hit on, but then, you just pulled in yesterday. If he'd been behind the desk when you arrived, he wouldn't have missed the chance to make a lewd remark or two in your direction."

"What does—did—his wife say about his shenanigans?"

"Rhonda?" Bea's eyebrows knit. She shook her head as she studied her cooling coffee. "That woman makes a good case for remaining single. She probably thought his flirting with everything in a skirt was cute when they were dating. Probably expected it to stop after they walked down the aisle. Why she stayed with him, I'll never understand. Must have been good in the sack because he sure as hell wasn't much to look at, and his personality sucked."

I hid a smile behind my mug. "Tell me how you really feel."

Bea's laughter startled a pooch out taking his owner for a walk. "Sorry. I camp here for a few weeks every year for the Ren Faire. There are other campgrounds, but this one is closest to the fairgrounds. I can ride my bike there without getting on any major roads."

Lots of campers had bicycles for puttering around the campgrounds. Bea kept hers chained to one of the camper's wheels with a cable long enough to allow her to park the bike underneath her awning.

"Ren Faire?"

"Renaissance Faire," Bea clarified. "People dress up in costume and pretend they're back in the Middle Ages. Hired actors play the parts of village locals and put on staged events, such as jousting matches and trials. You can get a giant grilled turkey leg to gnaw on as you walk around or a meat pie. All the food vendors are themed. It's a real hoot. You should go."

A loud bang came from inside the trailer. I sighed. "If I'm not in jail." I sipped my coffee.

"They're not going to find anything," Bea asserted. Leaning close, she spoke in a conspiratorial whisper. "Are they?"

I thought about the purse at my feet. "Nope."

CHAPTER FIVE

I waited until the police cars were out of sight before I examined the mess they'd made during their search. "They're idiots," Mason declared. "They didn't pull the drawers all the way out or anything." Clearly, he'd watched them like a hawk.

"Why would they do that?"

"Because that's the kind of place criminals hide stuff they don't want to be found."

"But, if people like you know that…wouldn't that make it a less than desirable place to hide things?" I stripped the sheets off the bed and tossed them into the mesh bag I used for dirty clothes.

Mason shrugged. "Criminals don't tend to be as smart as you, Vi. They do stupid stuff."

It was my turn to shrug. "It's not like they were going to find anything anyway. They're wasting their time. I didn't kill that man." I opened my lingerie drawer and tossed everything into the laundry bag. The thought of wearing intimate apparel that strange men had touched made my skin crawl.

"The question is, who did?" Mason pointed to the sink. "They took your favorite mug."

I turned to look. Sure enough, the bright yellow smiley face mug I'd left in the sink overnight was gone. "Shit! Why'd they do that?"

"Fingerprints. DNA."

I glared at my husband. "I didn't kill Ned! I didn't even know him!"

"You'd better find out who did before they pin this on you, Vi."

"How am I supposed to do that?"

I'd never thought his shrugs were annoying until now. "Ask questions. Figure out who had a motive to kill him. At the very least, you need to point the finger at someone else because I don't think those yahoos have the bandwidth to come up with another suspect."

"Bea said Ned hit on all the single women and some of the married ones."

"Then I'd start with his wife. Maybe she was tired of his philandering ways and put an end to them. Could have been the husband or boyfriend of some woman he hit on."

"Those both sound more likely than me being the killer. Why wouldn't the police be looking there instead of searching my stuff?"

"That's a good question, Vi. Something is definitely wrong here."

I gathered my laundry. "I'm going to walk down to the laundry room. While I'm waiting for the wash to finish, I'll stop in at the office and have a word with the widow. Express my condolences."

When I walked into the campground office, the widow Haggerty fixed me with a murderous glare.

The woman's narrowed eyes appeared clear as day and showed none of the signs of a recent bout of tears I had grown accustomed to seeing in the mirror in the days and weeks following Mason's untimely demise. No blotchy skin. No puffy eyes. No Rudolph nose from overuse of tissues. Mrs. Haggerty's hair and makeup were flawless, just as they'd been the day I checked into the campground. I mentally shrugged. Everyone handled grief in their own way, so who was I to judge? By all standards, the widow was a beautiful woman—when she wasn't glaring daggers at someone. "You need to leave. As a matter of fact, your reservation has been canceled. I want you out of here ASAP. I can't have a murderer on the premises."

I approached the desk with caution. "I'm really sorry for your loss, Mrs. Haggerty."

Surprise flickered in the woman's eyes before she narrowed them again and resumed glaring at me. "I recently lost my husband as well, so I know what you're going through. I wouldn't wish that kind of pain on anyone."

"Did you kill *him*, too?" Mrs. Haggerty's sneer was as sharp as icicles and just as cold.

"Mason died in an automobile accident."

"Are the authorities sure about that? Maybe you cut his brake lines, or…" She didn't seem to be able to come up with another possible scenario, so I butted in.

"I had nothing to do with my husband's death or yours. All I did was go for a walk. I wasn't paying close enough attention and slid off the trail. By the way, you should consider installing some railings. I could have been seriously injured if your husband's boot hadn't stopped my slide. Again, I'm sorry for your loss, but in an odd way, I'm grateful Mr. Haggerty was there to prevent me from tumbling to the bottom of the ravine. Good day, Mrs. Haggerty." I was almost to the door when I stopped and turned to the grieving widow. "The police told me to stay put until they complete their investigation, so I won't be leaving anytime soon."

The slap of the screened door against the frame felt like the perfect exclamation point on my parting words. How dare that woman insinuate I had played any part in Mason's death? My hands shook with anger as I transferred my clothes into the commercial dryer. It took two tries to feed the coins into the machine. Once it was going, I stared at the clothes through the viewing glass. The hum of the machine and watching the colorful items being tossed about helped calm my nerves.

The longer I watched, the more I thought about my encounter with the widow Haggerty. Sure, everyone dealt with grief in their own way, but unless Mrs. Haggerty knew some miracle cure to erase the signs of a crying jag, the woman hadn't shed a tear over her husband's demise. What kind of woman didn't cry over their dead husband? Especially when said husband had been murdered? It didn't make any sense.

Unless Mrs. Haggerty wasn't sad about Ned's death. Maybe Ned wasn't the only one stepping outside of the marriage. Perhaps Mrs. Haggerty conspired with her lover to eliminate her husband. I had never understood why someone would murder their spouse just to get out of their marriage when a divorce would be much simpler and didn't carry the threat of imprisonment. But I'd never been married to a philanderer.

CHAPTER SIX

"Are you alright, Violet?" Queen Bea called out from the shadow of her awning. I could just make out her figure sitting in a camp chair next to the cold fire pit. "I've got a fresh pot of coffee if you'd like some."

"That sounds good, Bea. Let me put my laundry away, and I'll be right over." I opened the door to my trailer. Before entering, I turned back. "Can I bring anything?"

"My sweet tooth is acting up. Got anything to make it feel better?"

I smiled at the older woman's antics. "I might. Let me look."

The beauty of living in a camping trailer was the lack of excess. I had just enough belongings to get by, so it only took a moment to put my freshly laundered clothes away and remake my bed. A quick search of my cabinets revealed an unopened package of donut holes I'd impulsively picked up on my last grocery shopping adventure. One of the things I liked about my frequent moves was trying out local brands and regional favorites. Even though I didn't need the calories, the apple cider donut holes had called my name. Sharing them with Bea would lessen my guilt over buying them.

I grabbed the bag of treats and reached for my favorite coffee mug, only to remember the police had taken it. Sighing, I opened the cabinet above the coffeemaker. There, front and center, sat Mason's favorite mug.

"Go ahead, Vi. Take it."

My hand trembled as I reached for the misshapen, hand-thrown mug emblazoned with the letters F.B.I. In parentheses underneath were the words "Full. Blown. Idiot." His sister made the cup for him as a gag gift for his fortieth birthday, and it instantly became his favorite. "I remember the day you got this." I smiled at the memory. "You laughed until your sides hurt. Olivia was so pleased with herself."

"And she'd be pleased to know you're using it now. You should take a selfie with it and send it to her."

"Maybe I will." I slipped my phone into my back pocket and grabbed the donuts off the counter. "I'll be careful with it. I promise."

"It's only a cup, Vi." Maybe it was to him, but to me it meant so much more.

I crossed the invisible line between campsites. I set the bag of treats on the side table next to Bea. "I brought donuts and my own mug,"

"Coffee's inside. Help yourself."

"Thanks. Try the donuts. Let me know if they're any good."

The layout of Bea's trailer was much the same as mine, but that's where the resemblance ended. Mine was spartan, but Bea's was filled with things the woman had collected in her travels. A dishtowel sporting the National Park logo and a picture of Old Faithful in Yellowstone hung from a towel bar beside the sink. Barrel-shaped salt and pepper shakers from Niagara Falls sat beside the small cooktop. Everywhere I looked, another souvenir, another memory, met my eye. I filled my mug and then joined my new friend outside to enjoy what was left of the afternoon. "Is there any place you haven't been?" I asked as I sat in the woman's spare chair. "Your trailer is like a roadmap of your travels."

"As you can see, I like to collect things that remind me of the places I've been. Some people would say my trailer is cluttered, but this trailer and my memories are all I've got."

There was a story there, but I didn't know her well enough yet to ask questions. Instead, I kept it simple. "I think it's wonderful. I haven't been anywhere I'd want to memorialize yet, but I think I'd like to start my own collection someday."

Bea bit into a donut. She made an appreciative sound as she chewed and swallowed. "Damn, those are good. Where did you get them?"

I helped myself to one. As we ate and drank our coffee, I told Bea about the Amish grocery store I visited on my way to my present campsite. "I could have filled the trailer with goodies, but restricted myself to the basics and these donuts."

"What about that mug? It looks handmade. Did you get it there, too?"

"No." I related the story behind the mug. "I probably never would have used it if the police hadn't taken my favorite mug when they searched my trailer this morning."

"They took your mug? Whatever for?"

I shrugged. "Fingerprints? DNA? I don't know. Maybe one of them collects things with smiley faces on them." I chuckled at my attempt at a joke. "My kids gave me that mug for Christmas when they were practically babies. Bought it at one of those holiday markets the schools hold as a fundraiser. I didn't want to take it on our trip, but Mason insisted our coffee wouldn't taste right if we didn't drink it out of our favorite mugs." I lifted Mason's mug. "He was right." I took a sip. "I hope they give it back soon. I'd hate to lose it forever."

"What's that one say?" She squinted to read the crude lettering. Olivia's pottery skills had improved since she'd made Mason's mug, but the glazing on this early attempt spoke to her amateur status.

I explained. "Would you take a picture for me? I'd like to send it to my sister-in-law." I handed over my phone and then posed with the mug at my lips while Bea took a series of photos. Examining them, I thanked the older woman, then sent a couple to Olivia and one to my kids. Elle and M.J. would be grateful for the proof of life. They'd understood why I wanted to get away, but they worried for my safety. If they knew I was under investigation for murder, they'd come running. Because they had their own lives, I elected to keep the murder rap to myself. Besides, it was all a bunch of hooey, anyway. The local police wouldn't charge me for something I didn't do.

CHAPTER SEVEN

"Don't say anything, Vi."

I could barely see Mason's apparition through my tears, but I heard his voice as clear as if he were standing right in front of me. But he wasn't. The local police detective, Ray Donaldson, recited my Miranda Rights as he cuffed my wrists behind my back.

"Use your one phone call to call Kurt Landis. He'll know what to do."

I nodded, letting my protector know I heard and understood. Kurt and Mason had been partners for over a decade. As friends go, they don't come any better. Like Mason, Kurt obtained his law degree from Harvard before joining the FBI. He didn't practice, but he'd be my champion.

Bea rushed up, pushing a uniformed officer out of the way before he could stuff me into the back of his patrol car. "Move aside, Barney Fife." Unsure what to make of the woman, the officer stepped back, allowing Bea to get in front of me. She dabbed at the tears on my cheeks and then held a tissue to my nose. "Blow, dear. You want to look your best in your mugshot."

The statement was so outlandish, I couldn't help but laugh. Gallows humor, I supposed. "Thanks, Bea. Don't worry. I'll be out soon." I didn't want to call Kurt, but I would if I had to.

The older woman nodded enthusiastically. "I know you will, honey. Don't you worry. We'll get you out of there! I promise!"

Seeing what was going on, Detective Donaldson wedged himself between me and Bea. "Move away." With a hand on the top of my head, he folded me into the cruiser and shut the door.

"You remember Kurt's number, right?"

I opened my mouth to reply, then thought better of it and nodded instead. If the police caught me seemingly talking to myself, they'd peg me as a lunatic as well as a murderer. Maybe I was crazy. I held regular conversations with the ghost of my dead husband. If that didn't constitute crazy, I didn't know what would.

As if he'd read my mind, Mason piped in, "You aren't crazy, Vi."

I refused to look at the apparition occupying the seat beside me. Of course, *he'd* say I wasn't crazy.

***

Detective Donaldson sat across from me in the tiny room that looked more like a broom closet than an office. It was complete with ugly industrial-grade carpet, a utilitarian metal desk, and two chairs. The detective occupied the ancient leather desk chair while I got the hard plastic one. Red lights on cameras mounted high in all four corners of the room replaced the two-way mirrors commonly featured in TV crime dramas. Everything I said or did would be recorded and used against me, so I sat as still as possible and waited for Donaldson to speak.

"Why'd you kill Ned Haggerty, Mrs. Hartwell?"

It was a great opening line. One designed to elicit an impassioned response. I wanted to respond, but knew better than to take the bait. I hadn't been married to an FBI agent for twenty-nine years without learning a few things. Digging deep for control, I uttered the one sentence Mason would approve of. "I want to speak to my lawyer."

The detective shook his head as he gathered his notes and case file into a neat stack, then stood. "Have it your way, Mrs. Hartwell. Someone will bring you a phone in a few minutes."

As soon as the door closed behind him, my shoulders fell, and my spine curved. A cool breeze brushed my shoulder, a subtle reminder that I wasn't alone. My left hand automatically went to my right shoulder, acknowledging Mason's touch. A few minutes passed before a policewoman brought in an old-fashioned push-button phone. After placing it on the table in front of me, she plugged it into a phone outlet on the wall.

"You're allowed one call, so make it a good one. Dial 9 for an outside line, then your number. You've got three minutes once the call connects." She placed a business card on the table. "Give your lawyer the address on the card."

I waited until the woman left before I closed my eyes and took a deep breath. With Kurt's private number clear in my mind, I brought the handset to my ear. It rang so many times I was sure my call would be sent to voicemail. Just as I was about to lose hope, the line clicked. I gripped the handset and prayed I wouldn't have to leave a message.

"Kurt Landis."

The familiar voice made me tear up, but I forced the sentimentality away and spoke up. "Kurt, it's Violet. I need your help. I've been arrested for murder."

The line was quiet for a second, and then Kurt's deep voice came back on the line. "Tell me where you are, Violet." I recited the information from the card the officer had left. "Sit tight and don't say anything. Not a damn thing. Do you hear me?"

"I hear you. Please hurry, Kurt."

"I'm on my way."

The line went dead, and I lowered the handset back to its cradle.

The hours ticked by in slow motion. The holding cell had no windows, and without a clock, I couldn't tell you if it was day or night. I sat on the thin mattress provided while Mason paced, sometimes outside the bars, sometimes inside. Watching him was as fascinating as it was comforting. I didn't dare speak to him. Nothing good could come of that. He'd warned me in the back of the cruiser that I'd be under video surveillance from here on out. If I started talking to myself, I'd be subject to a mental evaluation before the arraignment. Again, nothing good could come of that.

Mason stopped his pacing to face me. "Focus on something besides me, Vi, and just listen." For lack of anything better to look at, I stared at my feet, now clad in prison-issue slippers. They didn't have my size, so these were two sizes too big. With my back against the wall, my feet hung off the bed, and the oversized shoes dangled from my toes, flapping against my heels when I flexed my foot. Walking in them was a whole other experience.

"That's good, Vi." Just hearing his voice helped ease the anxiety, making my blood pressure skyrocket. "I eavesdropped on Detective Donaldson and his police chief. Let me tell you, the chief is a piece of work. I wouldn't trust him as far as I could throw him." Mason was an excellent judge of character. If he didn't trust the man, then the man had to be corrupt—just my luck. "They're planning to charge you with murder, but their evidence is all circumstantial. Number one—you were there. That's opportunity. Number two—you argued with his wife about the campsite you'd been given. That's motive. As for means, they don't have the murder weapon, so that's one in your favor."

Unable to verbally argue with Mason, I gazed at my feet and shook my head. Yes, I was there, but obviously, someone else had been there before me. Yes, I'd argued with the lady at the check-in desk about the assigned campsite. We'd booked a pull-through site. What we got required me to back the trailer in. Something I wasn't good at and wasn't in any hurry to get good at. As for the weapon, all my knives had been present and accounted for until the search team confiscated them. The only blood they'd find on them belonged to me.

"Tell Kurt everything. He'll make a hash of their flimsy case, and you'll be out of here in no time."

CHAPTER EIGHT

Kurt was a sight for sore eyes. Mason smiled as his best friend and work partner wrapped me up in his arms and held me while I cried. This time, the salty drops were joyful ones at seeing a familiar face. "Thanks for coming," I said, as I dabbed at my cheeks with the tissues Kurt drew from the pocket of his suit coat.

"What's this all about, Violet?"

He took my hand in his, anchoring me. I glanced up, catching the frown on Mason's face. I withdrew my hand, and Mason's approving gaze met mine. What was up with that? Squaring my shoulders, I turned my attention to Kurt and told him everything I knew, which wasn't much. "I didn't even know the man, Kurt. I had no reason to kill him. Not that I would have anyway. You know me. I escort spiders outside rather than stomp on them."

"You're one of the kindest people I know, Violet. Hang in there. We'll get you out of here in a jiffy."

My life had become a nightmare. I'd lost my husband, abandoned my home and what remained of my family, and now I was being accused of murdering a complete stranger. I stood beside Kurt in the courtroom in an orange jumpsuit that, like the slippers, hung off my body. If I'd had a dozen pillows to stuff inside, I'd have looked like the great pumpkin. Orange is not my color. Kurt oozed success in his bespoke suit and his pricey haircut. Mason looked good in a suit, too, but with a family to support, he bought his at a large retailer that specialized in menswear. Our local tailor fitted them to his physique for a lot less than what Kurt spent on his suits.

Detective Donaldson passed by on his way to sit with the

prosecuting attorney just as the judge entered the chambers. The charges against me were read—murder—as expected. I stood and, in as strong a voice as I could muster, declared myself not guilty. The judge studied the paperwork for a few moments, then addressed the prosecutor. "This is all circumstantial, Mr. Powers. And not very compelling. What have you got to say for yourself?"

Powers stood. "Your Honor, as stated, we believe Mrs. Hartwell, in a fit of rage over her assigned campsite, followed Mr. Haggerty and confronted him with a knife. After stabbing him multiple times, she left him for dead."

"But, it says here that she was the one who called 9-1-1."

"Yes, Your Honor. We believe she made the call to deflect suspicion from herself."

Kurt rose. "Your Honor, the prosecution has no evidence placing a knife in my client's hands. In fact, they've yet to recover the murder weapon, and when emergency responders arrived, no blood was found on Mrs. Hartwell's hands or clothing. Then, there's the fact that she'd never met Mr. Haggerty. In fact, she'd only caught a glimpse of him when she checked in and thought he was a maintenance man. To suggest she'd retaliate against a maintenance man because she didn't receive the campsite she was promised is ridiculous. Mrs. Hartwell is the widow of a career FBI agent who recently died in a tragic accident, as well as a dedicated individual who has devoted her life to her family and numerous charitable organizations in her community. I respectfully asked that these fabricated charges be dropped."

"Hmm." Seconds ticked by as the judge reviewed the case.

"Patience, Vi." Mason's calm voice brought a fresh bout of tears to my eyes. The judge would see how ridiculous this all was. He had to.

At long last, the judge glanced at the prosecutor. "Mr. Powers. I expect you to do better than this when this goes to trial."

What?

"Mr. Landis, the prosecution has requested bail be set at one million dollars. That seems excessive given the evidence presented so far. Not to mention, the ladies' facilities at the county lockup are under renovation. With those things in mind, bail is being set at one thousand dollars."

I stood on shaky legs as the judge exited the courtroom. When had my life become a real-life nightmare?

"Steady, Vi."

Steady? Mason had to be kidding. I felt like I was on one of those carnival rides that spin around until you're pinned to the wall—then the floor drops out from under you. My life had spun out of control the second Mason's car had left the pavement and careened into a tree. Then the floor dropped out from under me when I'd been arrested for murder. I'd hoped the ride would stop today and I could get off, but apparently, I was stuck on the hellish carousel for another go round.

Kurt clasped my cold, clammy hand in his. The warmth of his skin against mine instantly reminded me of the way Mason liked to hold my hand any chance he got. Oh, how I missed that simple human contact. Remembering Mason's reaction earlier when Kurt had taken my hand, I extracted my hand. Kurt didn't seem to notice the loss of contact. "Don't worry about the bail money, Violet. I'll cover it. When this is all over, you can pay me back. Until then, keep your funds in case you need them."

I forced my thoughts back to the proceedings. We stood in the courtroom as it emptied. A couple of uniformed officers waited to escort me back to the holding cell. Grasping at civility, I said, "Thank you seems inadequate." Kurt had come to my rescue and never once complained about the inconvenience or questioned my innocence. Thankfully, my bail was low enough I could pay it and still eat. "I can pay, Kurt."

Kurt let go of my hand and wrapped me up in a tight hug. "Let me do this for you, Violet."

"No need!" A now-familiar voice rose from behind. "We've got you covered."

Kurt's arms fell away, and I stepped back. Had that hug lasted just a tad too long? Or been too intimate? I shook the ridiculous thoughts from my head as my gaze met Queen Bea's. "What are you doing here, and what do you mean, you've got it covered?"

"Bail, honey. You didn't think we would let you rot in jail, did you?" She gestured to the back of the room where her entourage waited. The women who had recently become my friends smiled and waved. I forced my lips into something I hoped resembled a smile and waved back.

"Violet? Who is this?" Kurt's tone conveyed his distaste for the older woman. He lifted his chin to include the gathering at the back of the room. "And who are they?"

I introduced Bea. "She's a friend. And so are they." I flashed a grateful smile and a tiny wave at my newfound friends. "We're all at the same campground."

"You should move into a hotel until this is over. I can get someone to drive your truck and that ridiculous trailer back to your house. I told Mason he was crazy when he bought that thing."

"That won't be necessary, Kurt. I'll be fine in my trailer. I've got all these people watching out for me." Which was more than I could say about my friends and neighbors back home. I'd kept in touch via social media, but few had asked about my travels. Mostly, they'd asked when I planned to return, listing this fundraiser or that event as reasons I should come home. If I never attended another stifling function, it would be too soon.

I had always liked Kurt, but there was something about his tone that grated on my nerves. I'd expected him to be more supportive, but like my other friends, he didn't understand why I'd left. He'd been Mason's friend before he was mine, but he had no right to question Mason's decisions. Or mine, for that matter.

"The trailer was *our* dream, Kurt. Mason's *and* mine. We wanted to see the country, and not through hotel room windows."

Kurt placed his hands on his hips and leaned down so his gaze met mine. "I didn't want to say anything because you've been going through a lot, but I think Mason was having a midlife crisis or something. Why else would he buy a trailer and talk you into a cross-country camping trip?" He straightened; his gaze fixed on something far off as he swiped a hand over his mouth. I was about to tell him to save his breath when his gaze landed on me again. "Look, Violet, I think it's possible Mason drove off the road on purpose."

"What?!" I staggered back, catching myself against the sturdy wooden desk as my knees buckled. The female officer waiting to take me back to the holding cell rushed up to steady me. I held my hands out, wrists together. "Get me out of here. Please?" As the officer snapped the cuffs around my wrists, I called out to Bea. "I'll pay you back as soon as I'm out of here."

"Don't you worry, honey. We'll have you out in no time."

"Violet," Kurt pleaded. "I shouldn't have said anything."

"Thanks for coming, Kurt, but I've got it from here."

I'd never once entertained the idea that Mason had deliberately driven off the road. The idea was more than preposterous. It was…unfathomable. Mason would never have done something like that to himself or to his family. Why Kurt would believe such a thing made no sense. Truth, I thought as they led me away, nothing had made sense lately.

CHAPTER NINE

"I can't thank you enough." I hugged Bea. The older woman pushed out of my embrace with a chuckle. "I'll pay you back for the bail bond."

"You're one of us now. We couldn't let you rot in jail for something you didn't do."

I dabbed the corners of my eyes, willing the tears away as I smiled gratefully at the women assembled around the firepit in front of Bea's trailer. For the first time since Mason's accident, I didn't feel alone. "Really, ladies. You don't know how much this means to me."

"I think I do." Millie, the youngest of the bunch, spoke up. "These women were there for me when no one else in the world was. They're family now."

Kendra dug into a canvas tote slung over the back of her camp chair, then handed me a slightly crumpled but clean tissue. "There are two types of families. The one you're born with and the one you choose. You couldn't have chosen a better one."

The others expressed their sentiments individually, welcoming me into their tight-knit family. I'd never felt more at home. I breathed deeply and exhaled my pent-up stress, fears, and loneliness.

We passed around a bottle of cheap wine. Cups were filled as we settled into a comfortable circle around the fire. Willa was the first to speak. "So. Who was the hottie in the expensive suit?"

"Hottie?" It took me a few seconds to figure out who Willa was talking about. Then it dawned on me. "You think Kurt's a hottie?" He cut a dashing figure in a suit, but he'd always paled in comparison to Mason.

"She's talking about your lawyer," Bea clarified, giving Willa a raised eyebrow. "That one's always on the lookout for her next hookup."

"I am not!" Willa grinned. "But a girl can look, can't she?"

I chuckled at the younger woman's cheekiness. "Yes, you can look, but I'll warn you, Kurt's not the settling-down type. I don't think he's ever been with any woman for more than one night."

"Sounds like my type of man." Willa poured more wine into my tin spatterware cup. "I've never met a man I wanted to keep for more than one night." Cheers and laughter followed her brash statement.

I wiped tears of mirth from my cheeks. I could totally see Willa kicking Kurt out of her trailer at dawn. Just the idea of Kurt inside a trailer sent me into another fit of laughter. He'd made his stance clear on trailers and camping, though I didn't understand his aversion to the nomadic lifestyle. Recalling his disdain, I sobered. "Kurt offered to have someone tow my trailer away for me."

My circle of new friends went quiet.

"Why would he do a thing like that?" Bea asked.

"Tow it to where?" Kendra added.

"He said he'd have it towed home, but I don't think he meant to my house. He seemed to think Mason—that's my late husband—was having a midlife crisis or something, and had dragged me into it. He couldn't have been further from the truth. Owning an Airstream and seeing the country was our dream. It was just shitty luck that Mason was killed in a car accident the day before we planned to leave on our first adventure."

There was more silence as my new family digested my words. I couldn't get Kurt's dismissive attitude or his parting words out of my head. "Kurt has been a good friend to me and Mason for nearly two decades. I know I shocked a lot of people by leaving home so abruptly, and on my own, but Kurt shouldn't have been that surprised. I'm certain Mason talked to him about our plans, but he acted like I wasn't thinking clearly or something." Even worse, he'd insinuated that Mason hadn't been thinking clearly. He might have been Mason's partner at work, but Mason had been my partner in life. I knew him better than anyone else.

"This is why I don't want a man for more than one night," Willa chimed in. "They think women can't make a single decision without their input." She threw up her hands. "Makes me crazy!"

"As interesting as this conversation is," Bea butted in, "we've got bigger fish to fry. We know Violet didn't kill Ned, so we need to figure out who did and get her out of this mess. Anyone have any ideas?"

"The wife. The spouse is always the number one suspect." Everyone nodded at Sherry's wisdom.

"She didn't seem too broken up over his death." I recalled my visit with the woman the day after her husband's body had been discovered. "I don't think she'd shed a tear over him. Everyone grieves in their own way, but you'd expect to see evidence of some tears, even if there was no love lost between the two. She was married to him, for goodness sake!"

"How long were they married?" Sherry asked.

"Not long, I think," Millie offered. "I heard someone in town talking about her a few weeks ago."

Everyone leaned forward. Kendra prompted. "What did they say?"

Millie sipped her wine before answering. "It was two women at the Cut n Curl. Locals. They seemed to know Rhonda pretty well. They seemed to think she married Ned for his money."

"What money?" Bea gasped. "Ned was as poor as a church mouse."

"That's what I thought." Willa continued her story. "Apparently, that's not true. Ned was a trust-fund baby. Ned Sr. was loaded. Old money, from what I could tell, but Ned's daddy invested wisely and turned a lot into a lot more. According to them, Ned owned most of this county, among other things."

I sat back, contemplating what I'd just learned. "Well, that explains the rock on Rhonda's finger."

"Yeah. I wondered about that. Figured it must be costume jewelry, but I guess not." Kendra reached for the wine bottle and refilled my cup.

"I'm no expert on jewelry," I supplied, "but it looked real to me."

"Did Ned have any children? Maybe one of them killed him for the inheritance."

"They'd have been better off killing Rhonda. Ned didn't seem like a spendthrift. His clothes weren't expensive, and he sure as heck wasn't spending any money on this place." Anyone could see the deferred maintenance on the campground was adding up. The paint was peeling off every building, and the roads had more craters than the moon. Half the machines in the laundry hut had Out-of-Order signs on them. "His wife, on the other hand, wears expensive clothes and jewelry."

"What I don't understand," Kendra said, "is why they lived here to begin with. If what Willa overheard is true, why would anyone with that kind of money live in a rundown campground?"

"I wasn't aware that they lived here," I said, pondering the news. "Actually, I didn't know Ned owned the place until the police told me. I thought he was a manager or something."

Sherry joined the conversation. "We need to find out who benefited from Ned's death." She held up one finger. "His wife." Another finger went up, along with one eyebrow. "Who else? Another relative? A child?" She glanced at the assemblage. "Any ideas?"

Heads shook around the firepit as they silently contemplated the question. Sherry leaned back in her chair. "Well, somebody needs to find out."

"I've already burned my bridge with Rhonda," I said. "She thinks I murdered her husband and is none too pleased with me, though, in light of this new information, she should be thanking whoever did it."

"It could have been a crime of passion. Ned was a philanderer, which doesn't rule out his wife as a suspect. It also creates a long list of angry husbands and boyfriends."

"Could have been a scorned woman," Bea added.

"True." Willa opened a bag of potato chips. After offering them around without any takers, she plunged her hand into the bag.

Kendra leaned in. "Maybe it was a crime of opportunity. Was he robbed? It could have been some ne'er-do-well looking for a quick buck. There are lots of unsavory types roaming those trails." She glanced at me. "You can't be too careful out there. You're lucky whoever did it was long gone by the time you came along."

I hadn't thought of that. A shiver ran down my spine. "You really think it could have been some random person?" I didn't like the sound of that. Chances of the police locating a transient hiker were slim to none, which left me as the primary suspect. It was a bone-chilling thought.

Bea reached for Willa's bag of chips, taking a handful for

herself before passing it back. She ate a large chip and then washed it down with a sip of wine before turning her attention to me. "Did the police say anything about Ned being robbed? Did they find any of his belongings on you or in your trailer?"

I shook my head. "They didn't search me at the scene. I had on workout clothes, so it was pretty obvious I didn't have anything on me. There wasn't any way to hide anything. They couldn't have found anything in the trailer because there wasn't anything to find."

Silence fell as they contemplated the situation. I stared at the fire, willing the flames to chase away the cold seeping into my bones. "You know," I said, "I don't think I was a suspect in the beginning. They didn't search me. They didn't check to see if I had blood on my hands or clothes. I don't think it's possible to stab someone without getting blood on your hands or clothes. So what changed? I can't imagine any judge would approve a search warrant for my truck and trailer without any evidence to suggest I was involved in Ned's death."

Another heavy silence fell over the group. Minutes passed before Millie broke the spell. "I don't know about the rest of you, but something's fishy about Violet's arrest. If we don't do something, she's going to be convicted of killing Ned."

"What can we do?" Willa asked.

"Find the real killer." Bea lifted her camp cup for a toast. "Who's with me?"

CHAPTER TEN

"Your friends are right."

Accustomed to my late husband's ghost appearing at odd times, I didn't bother turning around as I slipped into my favorite pajamas. "About what?"

"There's something fishy going on."

I sat on the edge of the bed and ran a brush through my hair, working out the tangles before braiding it. "We have a plan." Ready for bed, I pulled the covers back and settled in.

"I heard." This time, the voice came from what would have been Mason's side of the bed. My heart clenched at the sight of him stretched out on top of the covers, his hands clasped behind his head as he stared at the ceiling. "Under normal circumstances, you know I'd never suggest you get involved in a murder investigation, but I'm afraid Bea is right. For whatever reason, the local police have focused their attention on you. The only way you'll clear your name is to find the real killer."

I didn't disagree, but something else had been bothering me since the arraignment: "Why did Kurt try to talk you out of going on this trip?"

Mason rolled over, mimicking my posture. Hands folded beneath his cheek, his gaze met mine. "I don't know. I'm sorry he said that to you—made it seem like you were bowing to my will. He's been weird ever since I bought the trailer." He cleared his throat. "And let's be clear, Violet. You and the twins are, *were,* my life. I did not intentionally drive off the road. I would never do that to you, M.J., and Elle. Why Kurt would think such a thing, much less put that idea in your head, is beyond me."

"I'm going to find myself another lawyer. Kurt made me uncomfortable today. I know he's your best friend, and I've considered him a friend, too, but there was something off about him today. He wanted to put me up in a hotel so he could have the trailer towed home. Why would he do that?"

"I don't know, Vi." Mason's brows met in the middle, a sign he was perplexed. "I thought calling him was the right thing to do, but I'm not so sure anymore."

Knowing I couldn't reach out and comfort my husband was like a knife to the heart—a feeling I was all too familiar with these days. Gazing into his troubled eyes, I wondered if the pain of losing him would ever ease.

"Don't worry about me, Vi. I'm fine. You need to take care of yourself." His gaze softened, and a small smile tilted his lips up on one side. "Close your eyes and get some sleep. I'll be here keeping watch."

I closed my eyes. "My own personal watchdog. I like it."

***

Bright sunlight streaming through the window over my bed woke me the following morning. Finding the other side of my bed empty, I sat up and stretched. Movement near the kitchen drew my attention. Mason leaned against the refrigerator, his ankles crossed and his arms folded over his chest. "Good morning, Vi."

"Morning." I padded past him to the coffeemaker. I'd slept surprisingly well, all things considered, but the weight of everything hanging over my head had me dragging. Bleary-eyed, I placed Mason's favorite mug under the drip spout and waited for the life-giving brew to materialize. Once I'd taken my first sip, I focused on my dead husband's figure. "I know that look. What's with you this morning?"

"I think you need to get a dog."

"What?" His response was so startling that I jostled the mug in my hands. Hot coffee spilled over the rim and onto my fingers. "Ouch! Crap." I set the mug on the counter and ran cold water over my abused skin.

"I didn't mean to startle you."

I inspected my reddened skin. Thank goodness the burn wouldn't require medical attention, but it was going to hurt for a while. "Yes, you did. You had that look on your face, so I knew

40

something was coming. I just didn't expect it to be *that*."

"What did you think I was going to say?"

I patted my hair and then smoothed out a wrinkle in my pajama top. "I don't know. Maybe something along the lines of, *You look like hell this morning, Vi?*"

"You're beautiful, and you know it."

"I need a haircut, and there's not enough concealer in the world to hide the circles underneath my eyes."

"I see what you're doing. Changing the subject isn't going to work."

I took a sip of my cooling coffee. Cold caffeine was better than none at all. "I don't need a dog. I can hardly take care of myself these days. Three weeks on the road by myself, and I've been accused of murder. What would happen to the poor dog if I'm convicted?"

Mason shifted. His broad shoulders barely fit between the cabinets lining both sides of the camper. "You won't be convicted."

"Do you know something I don't?" I walked right through the apparition to get to the closet. Mason hadn't intimidated me in life, and he sure wasn't going to in death. "Because it's not looking good from where I stand."

"You're changing the subject again, Vi. You need a dog. Someone to keep you company, and to watch out for you."

"Isn't that what you're doing?"

"I don't know how long I'll be here, and I can't bark or bite."

The tenuous nature of Mason's existence added to the weight on my shoulders. I sighed as I grabbed clean clothes out of the tiny closet. "I'll think about it."

***

"You bought a lot of wine. Going on a bender?"

I kept my eyes on the road as I navigated away from the shopping center. Driving the ginormous truck necessary to tow the trailer was nothing like driving the compact car I'd had for years. "My new friends consume a lot of wine. I also bought snacks to share and enough food to keep me going for the rest of the week." Coming to a stop at a red light, I loosened my tight grip on the steering wheel. "I'm doing the best I can, Mason. Nothing has been easy since you drove off that road."

"I'm sorry, Vi. I don't know what happened, but one thing I

know for sure—I didn't do it on purpose. I'd never do that to you and the kids."

The light changed to green. I curled my fingers around the steering wheel and accelerated through the intersection. "I know that, and the kids know that. If that's why you're hanging around, then you can go rest in peace."

"Turn right at the next light."

"What? Why?" I slowed the truck. "That's not the way to the campground."

"I know."

I frowned, but cautiously made the turn. "What are you up to, Mason Hartwell?"

"Just looking out for you, Vi. Like always."

Mason remained quiet for a few blocks, and then a sign caught my attention. "Honestly, Mason? I told you I don't want a dog." Nevertheless, I turned into the parking lot for the local Humane Society and found a space in the far reaches of the lot where I wouldn't risk hitting any other vehicles. I'd gotten better at driving the behemoth truck, but parking it was still a challenge.

"Just go in, Vi. Look around. No one is going to force you to adopt a dog if you don't want to."

CHAPTER ELEVEN

"What are you going to call him?"

I eyed the black Labrador Retriever sprawled across my bed like he owned it. I'd expected him to be more circumspect about his new surroundings, but he'd made a beeline for my bed, hopped up, and fallen fast asleep within seconds of his arrival. "His shelter name was Bud. It sort of fits, don't you think?"

Mason chuckled. "If that's short for Big Unruly Dog, then yeah, it fits. I was thinking you'd pick something smaller. An ankle-biter that would bark at everything that moves. Instead, you picked a lazy hound."

"They said three other families looked at him and didn't want him. He needed a home, so I gave him one."

"You've always had a soft heart, Vi." Mason smiled at the snoring dog. "He's not going to be much of a watchdog."

"I don't need a watchdog. I've got you." I left my new companion sleeping on the bed and went to the truck to retrieve the purchases I'd made at the pet store. As soon as I brought the giant bag of dog food into the trailer, Bud jumped off the bed and, tail wagging, came to see what was going on. "Back off, Bud."

"He must be hungry."

I squirted dish soap into the two large bowls I'd purchased for my new companion. "Give me a minute, Bud." I scrubbed, then rinsed the dishes. I'd no sooner placed the filled bowls on the floor than the dog growled and ran to the trailer door I'd left open. "Bud! What in the world?" The hair on his spine stood on end as he peered menacingly out the door.

Mason shrugged, indicating he didn't know any more than I did. "Better see what he's all worked up about."

I approached the growling pooch. "What is it, boy? Huh?" I gripped his collar, then nudged him over a step so I could see who or what had him so upset. Detective Donaldson stood beneath my extended canopy, his hand resting on the butt of his holstered weapon. "Oh, it's you." I patted the dog on the head. "Stand down, Cujo." The black lab ceased growling, but he clearly wasn't convinced the man facing him was harmless.

"You got a dog?"

"A murderer is running free. It was either get a dog or a gun. Given my status as your prime suspect, I figured a dog was the better choice." Telling him I already had a gun and that I knew how to use it didn't sound like a good idea. Thanks to Mason reminding me to take my purse with me when they arrived to search the camper, the local police were none the wiser about my firearm, and I planned to keep it that way.

Donaldson nodded. His hand dropped to his side. "You named him Cujo?"

I smiled. "His name is Bud, but given his reaction to you, Cujo might be a better name for him."

A smile broke across the man's face, and a chuckle escaped his lips. If I hadn't had one hand on my dog and the other on the wall next to the door, I might have toppled over as the stern-faced LEO transformed into a devastatingly handsome man.

He should smile more often. No sooner had the thought occurred to me than another one took its place. "What are you doing here?"

The man sobered. "Just checking in on you. I heard your lawyer left town."

"He's a family friend. He came to help me out, but he had to get back to his job."

"FBI?"

"That's right."

"Can I come in so we can talk?" His gaze shifted uncomfortably to the dog at my side.

"Do you have a warrant?"

"No. I'm just here to talk."

"I don't need a lawyer to tell me that's a bad idea."

Donaldson braced his hands on his hips, one knee cocked in a relaxed stance. "I'm not here to trick you into saying something incriminating. In fact, I came to tell you that I don't think you're guilty."

"Careful, Vi. Cops lie all the time to get people to let their guard down."

I stepped onto the outdoor rug I'd placed beneath the canopy. Bud padded down the steps and sat on his haunches beside my left leg. I studied the man before me. About the same height and build as Mason, he was, by all measures, a handsome man. Recalling how his smile had put a twinkle in his green eyes and a dimple into his cheek, I wondered if he knew the effect he had on women. Judging by the frown lines carved deep into his face, he didn't smile often, so maybe he didn't know. *Interesting.* Bringing my thoughts back to the subject at hand—my freedom—I asked, "Then why haven't you dropped the charges?"

"I tried. Chief Dreyer refused."

"Why would he do that? You have zero evidence to suggest I had anything to do with Mr. Haggerty's death."

"Chief Dreyer wasn't forthcoming with his reasons, but I wanted you to know the case isn't closed as far as I'm concerned."

"I appreciate you letting me know. Will you continue to investigate?"

"As much as I'm allowed to. We're a small department and don't have the luxury of investigating closed cases—as a general rule." He looked at the rug beneath his feet like he'd never seen one before. I waited, sensing he was getting up the nerve to say something else. I wasn't wrong. "Look, Mrs. Hartwell. I don't know how much I'll be able to do, so it might be in your best interest to hire a private detective."

"To do what? I don't have an alibi for the time of death, and a private eye can't change that."

"No, but as you pointed out earlier, there's still a murderer on the loose. Evidence that someone else committed the crime would render your lack of alibi a moot point."

I nodded. "I see. So, what you're saying is, you aren't going to do your job, so if I want my name cleared, I'm going to have to find the murderer myself. Do I have that correct?"

The detective's face flamed at my dressing down. "Not you. A private detective. I'd never suggest a woman like you to hunt down a murderer."

"Oh, boy," Mason mumbled. "He shouldn't have said that."

"A. Woman. Like. Me." I enunciated each syllable through gritted teeth. "What, exactly, do you mean by that, Detective Donaldson?"

The detective had the good sense to take a step back, literally and figuratively. "Nothing. I…" he stammered. "Nothing. I'm sure you're extremely capable, but this person has already killed once. You shouldn't put yourself at unnecessary risk."

Fists clenched at my sides, I stared the man down. Sensing my anger, my canine companion stood on all fours, ready to pounce if the detective made a wrong move. "Thank you for letting me know where I stand, detective. I'll be sure to let you know when I figure out who actually killed Mr. Haggerty."

CHAPTER TWELVE

"What are you doing?" Mason sat at the small banquette table, while I mixed brownies in a bowl.

"I'm thinking. Can't you tell?" Ever since I'd been old enough to wield a wooden spoon, I'd found comfort in baking.

"What are you thinking about?"

"I'm wondering who killed Mr. Haggerty, and how I'm going to find this person."

"Donaldson was right. You need to hire a private detective."

I froze mid-stir as my gaze snapped to my dead husband's apparition. "Not you, too. Why does everyone think I'm incapable of taking care of myself? Kurt, then Donaldson, now you."

"You're the most capable woman I've ever known, Vi, but Donaldson was right. This person has killed once. They've got nothing to lose by killing again. You, on the other hand, have everything to lose. You have a rich, exciting life ahead of you."

Hearing the sincerity in Mason's voice, I resumed stirring. Once the batter was smooth, I poured it into a pan I'd prepared earlier and popped it into the oven. After setting the timer, I faced the ghost of my past life. "I'll lose everything anyway if I don't find the murderer. You heard the detective. The police chief considers the case closed. No one is looking for the real killer."

"Doesn't mean you have to do it."

"Yes, it does."

"At least call a P.I."

"Who needs a P.I.? I've got all the help I need right here."

"Whoa, there." Mason held up a hand like a stop sign. "I can't do any more than advise, and I advise you to hire a professional."

"I wasn't talking about you." I raised my chin. "I have Queen Bea and her drones."

"You can't be serious."

"I've never been more serious in my life. What does a P.I. do anyway? Ask questions? If people around here won't talk to the police, they won't talk to a P.I. either. But no one will think twice about answering questions from a bunch of nosey women."

"You might be right about that."

"I know I am." The more I thought about it, the better the idea sounded. Abandoning the dirty mixing bowl and spoon, I opened my closet door. Sensing there might be something coming his way, Bud ambled along the center aisle of the trailer, tongue out and tail wagging. "It's not your dinner time yet," I said as I sorted through the clothes on hangers. "Perfect!" I held up the black dress I'd borrowed from my sister for Mason's funeral.

"What's that for?"

"Ned's funeral is this afternoon."

"You can't go to his funeral!"

"Why not? I didn't kill him."

"There's a reason investigators attend victims' funerals. Murderers often show up because they think doing so makes them look innocent. A decent investigator will see right through the charade."

"That's exactly why I need to go. The actual murderer will probably be there pretending to pay their respects." I shoved the bag of dog food aside. After digging around for a while, I pulled out the black pumps that went with the dress. "Bingo!"

Mason groaned. "Since I can't talk you out of this, at least take someone with you."

"No worries. I'll have an entire entourage." I picked up my phone and typed out a message in the group chat with Queen Bea and her drones. Responses poured in immediately, making me smile. I hadn't felt like myself since the moment I'd been informed of Mason's accident. It felt good to be in charge of my life again.

As soon as the brownies were done, I clipped the leash onto Bud's collar and took him for a walk around the campground. I felt bad about leaving him alone all afternoon so I could attend the funeral, so a nice long walk was the least I could do for him. And it gave me time to think. I knew one thing for certain. I didn't kill

Ned Haggerty. That left a lot of uncertainty out there, and I didn't even know where to start to narrow my search down to find the actual killer. Hopefully, something would click into place at the funeral. Someone would stand out. Otherwise, I was at a loss as to how to find the murderer. If I got too close, would I put myself in danger? Maybe Donaldson and Mason were right about hiring a private investigator.

Bud stopped to do his business, and while I waited, I noticed we'd arrived at the trailhead for Heartbreak Trail. I scooped poop into a bag and tied it off, then we ambled over to the trash receptacle next to the kiosk with a map of the trail. After dumping the poo, I took a look at the trail map. I'd been so angry with Mason the day I found Ned's body that I hadn't cared where the trail went. All I wanted to do was hike until my brain shut down. I located the *You Are Here* star and then traced the marked path until I came to the approximate area where I'd found Ned, just shy of a designated lookout point. Huh. I bet that was a beautiful spot. Once my name was cleared, I'd have to check it out. Past the lookout, the trail meandered through what appeared to be deep woods where it intersected with a couple of short access trails before skirting the Renaissance Fairegrounds. I bent and rubbed Bud's ears. "Someone could have entered the trail at any of those points, Buddy Boy. But how would they know Ned was going to be on that trail at that precise time? Unless he was there to meet someone? I suppose that's possible." Straightening, I continued to study the map. According to the map legend, Heartbreak Trail was over fifteen miles long, extending well past the Fairegrounds. I located the Faire on the map, noting the small lake that separated it from an unidentified parcel of land.

The alarm I'd set on my phone alerted me that it was time to get ready for Ned's funeral. Letting Bud run to the end of the retractable leash, I followed him back to my campsite. Back in the air conditioning, we both had some water and a treat—a homemade dog bone for Bud that I'd purchased in the same Amish grocery store where I'd scored the apple cider donuts I'd shared with Bea, and a couple of mass-produced chocolate chip cookies for me. I took a quick shower and put on my sister's black dress for what I hoped would be the last time, then applied the bare minimum of makeup.

Rap. Rap. Rap. "You ready in there?" Bea called out.

"Be right out!"

CHAPTER THIRTEEN

"What are we looking for?" Millie looked like she'd stepped off the pages of *Funeral Chic* magazine. Outfits like hers didn't come off department store racks. For the first time, I wondered how much the young woman had taken her ex for in the divorce settlement.

"I don't know." I watched a group of mourners enter the small chapel where the funeral was to be held. None of them looked particularly suspicious. "Maybe anyone appearing more nervous than broken up over Ned's demise?"

"Sounds good to me." Bea adjusted the pink scarf around her neck.

As Detective Donaldson walked by, he raised an eyebrow at me and my little group standing on the lawn. Thank goodness he kept moving. I didn't want anyone else trying to talk me out of investigating Ned's murder. Once the detective was out of sight, I addressed my friends. "You go on in and find seats. Don't sit together. Scatter out. I'll wait until everyone else is inside, then I'll sneak in and sit at the back. It wouldn't do for the widow to see me."

"You think she'd cause a scene?" Sherry asked.

"I'd hope not, but she *does* think I killed her husband."

"If she's guilty, she might stage a public attack against you to deflect attention from herself." This came from Kendra, who wore a sequined dress more suitable for a nightclub than a funeral. At least it was black.

"Good point." I mulled that over. Mrs. Haggerty hadn't

seemed all that broken up over her husband's death when I had talked to her. "Let's keep an eye on her today. The spouse is always the number one suspect."

"Speaking of…" Willa lifted her chin, indicating something over my shoulder.

"Who's that with her?" Bea asked.

Kendra leaned to see around her. "They look cozy."

I waited until the couple turned onto the walkway leading to the front of the chapel. Indeed, they did look cozy. The widow Haggerty, dressed like she shopped at the same expensive boutique as Millie, approached the chapel on the arm of a man I didn't recognize. At least a dozen years older than the woman hanging off his arm, his off-the-rack suit could have used a good steaming before he put it on, and his shoes had traces of dried mud stuck to them. Did the woman have a thing for poorly dressed men? The one time I had seen Ned alive, he hadn't struck me as a man who cared much about his appearance. "Who's she with?"

My entourage shook their heads in unison. I nudged Millie with my elbow. "Go!" I whisper-hissed. "Scoot in behind them and keep your ears open. We need to know who that is."

The youngest of their group of busybodies power-walked across the lawn and fell into step a discreet distance behind the mismatched couple.

"If anyone can blend in and get the scoop on Mrs. Haggerty, it's Millie." Bea sounded confident, but I had my doubts.

"I don't know. If Rhonda gets a load of the way Millie's dressed, she may suspect her of sleeping with Ned. There aren't many campers who can afford designer duds."

Kendra snickered. "Ned must have been a god in bed."

"Why would you say that?" The same question had been on my lips, but Willa asked first.

"I don't think he was handing out expensive gifts to get women to sleep with him, so he must have had something else his conquests wanted."

"How do you know he wasn't showering the women with gifts?"

Kendra's left shoulder rose and fell. "He was spending a lot of time with Millie's neighbor when her husband was off fishing, and by time, I think you know what I mean." She waggled her eyebrows. A chorus of *ohs* rose from the group. "Anyway, that was going on for at least a month, and I never saw any evidence she got anything out of him other than maybe an STD."

"Huh." Willa stared into the distance. "Is her neighbor still there, or did she pull up stakes after Ned was murdered?"

"She's still there. Her husband still goes fishing every day."

"We need to talk to her." I made a mental note to look the woman up when we returned to the campground.

"We can talk to her at the cemetery."

"What do you mean? Is she here?" My heart rate spiked. "What about her husband?"

Kendra tipped her head toward the sidewalk. "That's her. Camille's her name. Her husband's Earl, and I doubt he'd take time off from fishing for his own funeral, much less for his wife's lover's."

Checking her out in my periphery, I noted how young she looked. She couldn't be over twenty-five, and she was smartly dressed in a timeless black wrap dress and kitten-heeled sandals. She wore no jewelry, except for a wedding ring and the large gold clasp that held her blonde hair at the nape of her neck. If I had to name her style, I'd call it Classic. "She's not what I expected."

"What did you expect?" Bea asked.

I shrugged. "I don't know. Maybe someone older, less put together. Someone desperate for attention. She's dressed to blend in."

"She must have driven over to the mall in Philly to get that dress," Willa commented. "The stores in town don't sell anything that nice."

"It does look expensive," I mused. "Maybe Ned was paying his lovers after all."

Kendra hummed low. "We can ask her at the cemetery. Come on. The service will start soon. We need to go find our seats."

I waved them on. "I'll join you in a bit."

Bea held back for a moment. When the others disappeared inside, she touched my arm. "You don't have to do this. We've got it."

I took a deep breath and let it out. "Thanks, Bea, but I'll be okay. You go ahead. I'll be right behind you."

After Bea, in her black, floral print dress with the bright pink scarf, entered the chapel, I counted to ten, then made my way inside.

CHAPTER FOURTEEN

I sat next to the center aisle in the back row, ready to sprint out the door if the widow Haggerty or anyone else objected to my being there. The chances of that were slim, given that the only people I knew besides the widow were my friends from the campground and Detective Donaldson. Based on the look he'd given me before entering the building, the detective wasn't happy about my being here, but causing a scene wouldn't do him any good. That just left the widow to worry about, and I felt confident I could fly beneath the woman's radar.

I had been so wrapped up in crafting my plans that I hadn't taken into account how difficult it would be to sit through another funeral so close after Mason's. It didn't matter that I didn't know the deceased. The overpowering floral scent from the flower arrangements, the somber music, and the closed coffin up front brought back memories of the worst day of my life. As the last notes of the opening hymn faded and the minister took to the pulpit, I scooted into the aisle and fled to the vestibule, where I leaned against the wall and tried to calm my racing heart.

I'd been a wreck the day they laid Mason to rest. Hardly able to function. Unlike Ned's widow, I'd been crippled by grief and needed physical assistance to walk the few steps required.

As the minister quoted scripture and piped-in music signaled the start of another hymn, I thought about Rhonda Haggerty's arrival on the arm of the mystery man. If I hadn't known better, I would have thought they were out for a stroll in the park. Granted, everyone processed grief in their own way, so I wouldn't judge the widow too harshly on that account. Focusing on the reason I was there helped me push my own raw grief aside and allowed me to tune back in to the service just as the minister began a detailed recounting of Ned's accomplishments in life.

"Ned Haggerty was the beloved only child of Henry and Rose Haggerty, pillars in our small community. Ned leaves behind his wife, Rhonda, and daughter, Camille Stone."

Wait. What?

A gasp rose from the front row. The newly minted widow bolted up like someone had hit the eject button on her pew. The irate woman pointed a finger at the officiant. "She's no relation to Ned!" She spun to face the congregants, her gaze wildly sweeping the filled pews until she found the face she wanted. Camille sobbed into a linen hanky Millie passed to her. Her shoulders heaved with grief. If she wasn't Ned's daughter, she was a damned good actor. But weren't all con artists?

Venom spewed from the widow's lips. "You're nothing but a two-bit hustler! If you think for one second, I'm going to let you get away with this, you're dead wrong!"

Rhonda tugged on the sleeve of the man sitting next to her. The very same man who had escorted her into the chapel. "Harvey! Get. Up. Arrest her! Right now!"

Harvey remained in his seat. "Rhonda, honey, you know I can't do that. Sit down and let Reverend Timmons get through the ceremony. I promise I'll look into the claim as soon as Ned's in the ground."

I whispered to the woman sitting next to me. "Who's that?"

"Harvey Dreyer. He's the Chief of Police."

Oh. I straightened in my seat. He was old enough to be Rhonda's father. And the man who had declined to drop the charges against me. Interesting.

Rhonda plopped heavily into her seat and then glared over her shoulder at Camille, whose sobs had ended as quickly as they'd begun.

The officiant cleared his throat. As he adjusted his tie, he nervously scanned the room for more trouble. When no one else spoke up, he resumed his prepared remarks, talking about Ned's contributions to the community, including donating money for the new playground next to the elementary school and purchasing new instruments for the high school band program. Apparently, the man was quite the philanthropist. Nothing else came to light beyond the sudden revelation that Ned had a daughter, and there were no further interruptions.

Questions swirled in my brain. If Camille was Ned's daughter, then who was her mother? It sure wasn't Ned's widow. She wasn't old enough to have a child that age. Mind reeling, I quietly scooted out of the pew and retreated to the lawn while I waited for the service to conclude. Standing in the shade, I watched as everyone filed out of the chapel. Rhonda and her police escort followed the casket to the hearse. After Ned was loaded inside for the trip to the cemetery across town, everyone broke away to their respective vehicles. Camille, recovered from her bout of profound grief, got behind the wheel of the ancient pickup truck I recognized from the campground. Rhonda and Harvey followed the hearse in a chauffeur-driven limo with darkly tinted windows.

My friends gathered to watch the procession file past.

"I'd love to be a fly on the wall in there." Bea nodded toward the passing limo. "I bet Rhonda is fit to be tied."

I addressed the group. "Did any of you know Camille was Ned's daughter?" Heads shook all around.

"She never said a word to me." Millie's brows knit. "Honestly, I was sure she was having an affair with Ned. I almost fell out of the pew when Rhonda pointed a finger at Camille. She started bawling instantly. Up until then, she'd been as dry as the Sahara."

I dug my car keys out of my purse. "We should go to the cemetery. Things could get interesting there."

"More interesting than a long-lost daughter turning up at the funeral?" Kendra's dry humor made us all smile.

Sherry was the first to head toward the parking lot. "Come on," she called over her shoulder. "We don't want to miss anything."

Bea accompanied me across the lawn. "Do you think Camille could be Ned's daughter?"

"Beats me, but I guess it's possible."

"If it's true, that would be a motive for murder. She'd be entitled to a sizeable chunk of Ned's estate.

"And if she isn't the murderer, her inheritance would put a target on her back."

We stopped in front of my truck. Bea nodded. "*If* Ned was

murdered for his money."

"You're right, Bea. My late husband always said most murders involve either money or sex. Ned was a philanderer. Maybe he wasn't having an affair with Camille, but his exploits at the campground *were* well-known. We can't rule out a jealous husband or a scorned lover."

I got behind the wheel, and Bea situated herself in the passenger seat. It didn't take long to catch up to the procession. As it wound its way through the small town, people stopped on the side of the road to let it pass, many standing beside their vehicles with heads bowed and hats off.

When we arrived, the widow was already seated in the first row of chairs beneath the shade canopy. Camille occupied a seat at the end of the first row. The seats between Ned's widow and his alleged daughter were occupied, but from where I stood, I couldn't see much more than the tops of their heads. "Who are the other people in the front row?"

Bea shrugged and whispered back. "No idea. I don't recall seeing them at the chapel."

Mourners filled the chairs behind the grieving family while the overflow formed a protective wall around the tent. I recognized a few faces from my brief forays into town for supplies. Ned had been a part of this community his entire life, so it stood to reason that many of the townsfolk had known him. Was one of them the killer? Had Ned's philandering ways spilled over from the campground to the local residents? Had some jealous husband found out and put an end to Ned? Or maybe a scorned lover?

I stifled a sigh. I'd hoped attending Ned's funeral would help narrow down the suspects, but instead, I now had an entire town full of potential murderers to consider.

A tortured cry made the hair on the back of my neck stand on end. I glanced up in time to see Rhonda throw herself onto the casket. I knew that feeling. Knew it down to the marrow of my bones. As her companion placed his hands on her shoulder and tried to comfort her, I turned and made my way back to my truck. One thing I knew for sure. Rhonda Haggerty had not murdered her husband. Grief that deep couldn't be faked.

CHAPTER FIFTEEN

I climbed into the cab of my pickup and closed the door on the outside world. Dropping my forehead to the steering wheel, tears I'd held back flowed freely.

"I'm so sorry."

"Shut up, Mason." I dug a tissue out of my purse and blew my nose. "I know you're sorry, but that doesn't change anything. I'm still alone."

Bea knocked on the driver's side window. I pressed a button, and the glass slid down. "You okay?" the older woman asked.

"Just needed a minute." Taking a deep breath, I blinked tears away. "I'm coming."

"Take your time. We've got this."

I cringed at the pity in Bea's voice. Setting my grief aside, I pushed the door open and stepped out of the truck. "I'm good." I straightened my dress, taking another second to steady my nerves. Too much was riding on my investigation to let my grief keep me on the sidelines. "Is someone keeping an eye on the daughter?"

"Millie is watching her."

"Good." I took a cleansing breath and exhaled before I let my gaze wander back to the graveside. People were leaving, indicating that the service had come to a close. If I were going to speak with Camille, now was the time. "I need to talk to the daughter." I dug the truck keys out of my purse and handed them to Bea. "Take my truck. I'll see you back at the campground."

"Wait!" Bea called out.

I waved her off. Keeping to the shoulder of the narrow

blacktop road, I reached the older model pickup about the same time its owner did. Noticing the door wasn't locked, I opened the passenger side and slid onto the old bench seat just as Camille settled into the driver's seat.

As the younger woman turned to place her purse on the seat, she noticed me. Letting out a startled gasp, she yanked her purse back, clutching it to her chest.

I smiled at the woman. "You're Camille, right? I'm Violet Hartwell."

"You're the woman who killed my father."

"Actually, I'm not. I found his remains, but I didn't kill him."

"But…the police—"

"Are wrong. I had no reason to kill him. I didn't even know him."

"Then, why—"

"Why are they trying to pin it on me?" I glanced out the windshield. The lead cars began to move. "That's what I'd like to know." I nodded as the car in front of us eased onto the road. "Better get moving before the people behind us start honking."

Camille glanced in the rearview mirror, then back at me. "Where are we going?"

"The campground? I don't think either of us is welcome at the wake." Word had circulated that the widow would receive guests at the downtown community hall. All were invited to stop by for a bite to eat and to express their condolences.

"You're probably right about that." The old engine reluctantly cranked. Camille checked for traffic over her shoulder, then manhandled the dinosaur onto the pathway. We both fastened our after-market seatbelts before Camille pulled out of the cemetery onto the multi-lane road. She shifted into cruising gear as we headed out of town. "You're sure you didn't murder Ned?"

"Positive. And I'm guessing you didn't murder him either."

"No. I had no reason to want him dead. I'd just found my biological father after years of searching. He'd been nothing but gracious to me since we met. We weren't ever going to be super close, but I'd hoped we'd stay in touch."

"What about the money?"

"Money? Ned didn't have two nickels to rub together."

I raised an eyebrow. "That's not what I heard."

Camille's gaze snapped to me, then back to the road.

"Seriously? Who would say something like that?"

"Apparently, everyone in town knew. Ned inherited it all when his father died. Money. Land. Who knows what all?"

"He lived in an old camper in a rundown campground." She didn't even try to hide her disbelief.

I held both hands up in surrender. "Hey, I'm just telling you what I heard."

"It sounds like bullshit to me. Pardon my French." She pointed up ahead. "Mind if we stop by and pick my husband up? I dropped him off this morning so I could keep the truck."

I eyed the single bench seat. I really didn't think Camille or her husband had anything to do with Ned's death, but being stuck between them in the cab of their truck might qualify me for TSTL (Too Stupid To Live) status. "He didn't want to attend the funeral?"

"No. He said he'd go if I wanted him to, but he didn't really know Ned. Not that I did either."

"How did the officiant know you were Ned's daughter?"

Camille turned onto a dirt road. A lake glistened in the distance through the trees. "I don't know. I didn't tell him."

That was odd. I was certain the not-so-grieving widow wouldn't have mentioned Camille to anyone. Someone had wanted to stir up drama at the memorial service. But who? "Well, the news went over like a fart in a crowded elevator."

"Not my fault. I didn't know anything about Ned until a few weeks ago. I'd been searching for my biological parents for years. Then, all of a sudden, Ned popped up as a DNA match in my online profile. After I got over the shock of actually finding one of my parents, I contacted him, and he invited me to come for a visit so we could get to know each other."

"You said you've been searching for your biological parents. I take it then that you were adopted?"

"I was. Apparently, my birth mother abandoned me on the steps of a church in Philadelphia. The pastor's wife found me when she arrived to arrange the flowers for the early morning service. They were already registered as foster parents, so they took me in and later adopted me."

"That's an incredible story. I assume you asked Ned if he knew?"

"Of course. He claimed he didn't have any idea I existed, or he would have kept me."

"Did he say who your mother is?"

"No. He told me he thought he knew but didn't want to say anything until he talked to her."

"So, she still lives around here?"

"I suppose so."

"You could have met her and not even known it."

"I doubt it. The only people I've met since I arrived are at the campground. Ned introduced us to Rhonda as soon as Earl and I arrived."

"How did that meeting go?"

"About like you'd expect. Rhonda hated me on sight." Camille maneuvered the truck around a giant pothole, but hit the next one with a bone-jarring thud. She gave me an apologetic grin. "Sorry. I hate this road, but Earl says the best fishing spots are down this way." After a few more teeth-rattling dips in the road, the surface smoothed out, and we picked up speed. "I kinda expected Ned would have told Rhonda about me before I arrived, but that didn't appear to be the case. The woman was livid. She called Ned a bunch of unflattering names. She would have lit into me next, but a family came in to shop for supplies. Rhonda transformed from Grizzly Bear to Teddy Bear in the blink of an eye. The woman should be on stage."

"What do you do for a living, if you don't mind my asking?"

"I'm a romance author."

"Really?" I had become hooked on romance books when the twins were toddlers and had been an avid reader of the genre ever since. "Do you write under your real name?"

The younger woman's laughter filled the cab. "Goodness, no! That would be awkward."

I raised an eyebrow. "Oh? How so?"

"Promise you won't judge me?"

"Promise."

"I write Daddy Kink under the name Pink Sparkles."

"Daddy Kink?"

"You know, littles?"

I knew both terms. I was just having difficulty reconciling what I knew about the genre with the person driving. "I've read a few. They're not really my thing, but I've heard they're popular."

"You could say that. I've made over seven figures a year for several years, and my only expenses are the cost of printing the books I sell from my online store."

"I guess you don't need Ned's money then."

"Heck, no. Not that I believe he had any. I've got more money than I can spend in this lifetime."

My gaze swept the dilapidated truck. "Then why the old truck and the even older camper?"

"The camper was Ned's idea. I wanted to stay at a hotel in town, but Ned said he wanted me close so we could talk. The truck is Earl's next project. His hobby is restoring vintage trucks. We picked this one up at an auction on the way here." My butt came off the seat as Camille hit a moon crater, then cranked the steering wheel and navigated down another dirt road. "I don't usually drive anything bigger than a tricycle if it doesn't have power steering, seat warmers, and air conditioning."

I couldn't argue with that. Moments later, the lake came back into view. Earl sat on a rock outcropping, his line in the water. Recognizing the truck, he stood and reeled in his line. He gathered his belongings and met us when we came to a stop.

This was the first time I had seen the elusive Earl. He appeared to be the lazy bum everyone said he was. Yet, there was something familiar about the way he studied the approaching truck. I watched as he stowed his gear in the bed and then wrenched the driver's side door open. Camille scooted to the middle as he climbed in and cranked the engine. "How was the service?"

His wife sighed. "I wish you'd been there. That woman was absolutely awful to me."

Earl leaned around to give me the evil eye.

"Not me!"

Camille laughed. "Calm down, Earl. Violet's cool."

"Isn't she the prime suspect in Ned's murder?"

"She says she didn't do it, and I believe her." She sighed. "Rhonda was horrible. When the minister listed me as Ned's daughter, Rhonda shot out of her seat and told everyone that I'm an imposter."

Earl put the truck in gear, heading back the way we'd come. "Sorry, Violet." He placed a hand on Camille's thigh. "I'm sorry, honey. I know you were hoping for a better outcome from all this."

"It's okay. I feel sorry for Rhonda. Ned really loved her, and now he's gone. She has every right to be bitter."

"You're too generous, babe." He was better at missing potholes than his wife, but the ride was still jarring. "How did the minister know you were Ned's daughter? Did you tell him?"

"No! At first I thought Rhonda did, but when she jumped up and accused me of being a fraud, I figured she didn't do it."

"Then who did?" he asked.

"I have no idea. As far as I know, only Ned and Rhonda knew about me."

"Unless Ned confronted your birth mother."

"I guess that's possible, but why would she tell anyone? She obviously didn't want anyone to know about me back in the day, not even Ned."

"You make a good point," Earl conceded.

Camille bumped shoulders with her husband. "Enough about my dreadful day. How was yours? Catch anything?"

"Maybe." He motioned to the glove box. "Can you get my phone? I need to report in."

I shifted my knees toward the door, allowing room for the glove box to drop open. A sharp gasp escaped my lips when I spied the contents of the small storage compartment.

CHAPTER SIXTEEN

Camille casually reached beneath the black leather holster, her fingers searching for the slim phone hidden in the dark depths of the glove box. Seeing the holstered weapon brought back decades of memories. I was still processing what I'd seen when Camille found what she was looking for and slammed the container shut.

She held the device out. "Here you go."

The truck abruptly came to a halt in the middle of the dirt road. Earl jumped out of the cab. "Give me a minute. I'll be right back."

I turned in my seat to watch the man stride away from the vehicle. He eventually stopped a couple dozen yards away, his phone pressed to his ear. I turned back to Camille. "Earl's a cop?"

"What makes you say that?"

"You're shit at lying." I gestured to the glove compartment. "That's a service weapon. My husband had one just like it."

"Look, you can't tell anybody. Okay? Earl's here on a case. He wouldn't know what to do with a fish if he caught one. The whole fishing thing is a cover."

"What kind of case is he working on?"

"You'd have to ask him, but don't expect him to tell you. He never discusses his work with me."

I could relate to the frustration in Camille's voice. "Mason never told me anything either. But if his being here has anything to do with what happened to Ned, I need to know. I've got to clear my name, or I'm going to go away for life for something I didn't do."

"Some things are going on in the area that Ned might have been involved in."

"Like what?"

The driver's door screeched open. Earl climbed back in and put the truck in gear. "How about we go into town tonight for a burger?" he asked as if my world hadn't just shifted a few steps to the left.

Camille patted him on the arm. "That sounds good, honey, but Violet knows."

"Knows what?"

"That you aren't a lazy bum."

Keeping his eyes on the road ahead and his hands firmly on the steering wheel, Earl laughed. "What does Violet think I am? The CEO of a Fortune 500 company?"

I leaned around Camille so I could watch Earl's face. "You're a cop. Probably a federal agent. Either that or you stole someone's service weapon." Earl's eyes followed my hand gesture toward the weapon hidden behind the closed door.

"What makes you think that's a service weapon? I spend a lot of time out in the woods alone. Fishing. I don't like to be without protection."

I scoffed. "That's bullshit, and you know it. My late husband was in the FBI for over twenty years. That's a government-issued holster, and I'd bet my Airstream that the weapon inside it is, too."

Earl made a sharp turn onto a narrow dirt road. I glimpsed a sign indicating a picnic spot lay ahead, but before I could draw a breath to ask what was going on, the truck jerked to a stop next to a concrete picnic table covered in leaf debris. Talk about under-used facilities. This one looked like no one had taken advantage of its remote beauty in years. A shiver raced down my spine as Earl wrenched his door open and demanded, "Get out!"

"Better do as he says." Camille elbowed me in the ribs. "He's in damage-control mode."

I didn't want to know what that meant, but being trapped in the cab of an old pickup with Camille's sharp elbow wasn't an option.

As soon as my feet hit the ground, Earl reached into the cab. When he stepped clear of the door, he slipped the holstered weapon onto his hip with the ease of having done it a million times. The rigid stance and intense scrutiny of a trained professional replaced the slouched shoulders and blank expression. Yep. Fed. It was written all over the guy. He flipped open a leather wallet to reveal a gold and blue shield. "DEA," he said, by way of explanation.

I examined the badge. "That tracks."

"You can't say anything to anybody, Mrs. Hartwell."

I'd never compromise a LEO, but if Earl had information that could exonerate me, then I was going to use it. "The local authorities think I killed your wife's father, Agent Stone. They have no evidence, yet no one is looking for the actual killer. So, if you have any information that can clear my name, you have to tell the local police."

"If I knew something that would help you, I would have already gone to the locals."

"You're DEA," I stated. "That means drugs are involved. Was Ned involved?"

Earl's gaze darted to his wife, then back to me. "I don't know." His tone was almost apologetic as he turned his gaze back to Camille. "Maybe? But I honestly don't think so. He may have been in the wrong place at the wrong time."

"You think Ned stumbled on a drug deal and it got him killed?" Tears filled Camille's eyes. "Please tell me you aren't here investigating my father."

"Baby. No." Earl gathered Camille in his arms. "There's no indication he was involved in the drug trafficking. All I'm saying is, he might have heard, seen, or stumbled into something related that made him a target." He set her away from him, but kept his hands on her shoulders. Bending down to look into her eyes, he asked, "Did he say anything to you about strange things going on at the campground or the Ren Faire? Anything at all?"

Camille wiped tears off her cheeks. "No. I didn't even know he had money until Violet mentioned it when we were leaving the cemetery."

"Ned had money? What kind of money?" Earl's hard gaze landed on me. "How do you know this?"

"A friend of mine heard it in town. Ned's father inherited a little money and turned it into a lot of money. Apparently, Ned owned a lot of land in the county, including the campground and the property the Renaissance Faire leases. I got the impression that it wasn't a secret. Most of the townspeople knew. The officiant at the funeral mentioned Ned's generous donations to local charities.

If what they say is true, he didn't need drug money. He had plenty of his own."

Earl drew his wife close again. "I'll have someone check it out, honey. I hadn't seen anything to suggest his involvement in the trafficking, but if what Violet heard is true, then Ned's murder may have more to do with his personal fortune than my investigation."

Camille hugged her husband, then stepped away. "God, I hope someone didn't murder him for his money. According to the minister, Ned was a generous man. He probably would have given them something if they asked."

"Your wife is right. From all accounts, Ned didn't hoard his money." A thought occurred to me. "Camille, do you know if Ned had a will?"

She shook her head. "I have no idea. We didn't talk about finances, his or mine."

"I wonder who stood to gain by his death? Besides his wife, of course, and now, I suppose you're entitled to something."

"I don't need or want Ned's money. But you're right. If he had a will, it would be interesting to see who would profit from his demise."

At last, there was something tangible I could do that might lead to Ned's murderer. "We need to find out if he had a will, and if so, when it will be read."

"I can ask Rhonda," Camille offered. "She already thinks I'm a gold digger, so she won't think anything of me asking about a will."

"Whoa. Wait just a minute." Earl held a hand up like a stop sign. "I don't want you anywhere near this situation. Whether you are entitled to some of his money or not, just being his daughter could put a target on your back."

For the first time since Camille had revealed what she wrote, I saw why she made millions at it. Her gaze softened as she snuggled close to Earl. With a pout on her lips, she gazed up at him and, in a childlike voice, pleaded. "I'll be careful, Daddy. I promise. Please let me go?"

Behind me, Mason chuckled as Earl looked horrified at his wife's behavior. "Cut it out, Cammie." His gaze met mine. "Honestly, this isn't what it looks like."

"Oh? What do you think it looks like?" I was ninety-nine percent sure she was messing with him, but given what she'd told me about her writing, I couldn't be one-hundred percent sure.

The man was beyond exasperated as he stepped away from his wife. "Okay. Okay. But I'm going with you. Then I'm going to rent a car, and you're going home. I want you far away from everyone here."

Camille's demeanor changed on a dime, and she was back to being an adult. "Awesome! I knew you'd see it my way. Let's go."

"She's got him wrapped around her little finger." Mason chuckled as we piled back into the rust heap they called a truck and headed back to the campground.

CHAPTER SEVENTEEN

Camille and Earl joined the group around Bea's firepit that evening to discuss what we'd individually found out. After introducing our newcomers, I started us off. "Rhonda didn't kill her husband." I held up a hand to silence the naysayers. When I had everyone's attention, I continued. "I don't have any concrete evidence to support that statement, but I know what I saw today at the cemetery. I know that kind of grief, and it can't be faked." I met the flurry of questions with another staying hand. "I know. I know. I was quick to question Rhonda's lack of grieving, but what I saw today was real. Has anyone here lost a husband?" I nodded to Earl, "Or a wife?" A chorus of "No," and heads shaking. "Then I'm the only one here qualified to judge the woman's display. Let me tell you, reality can be a bitch. I don't think it hit her until today that Ned is really dead. Believe me, once that reality hits, the grief is overwhelming."

"I'm so sorry, Vi." Mason's voice held a world of pain. I hated that his death had cut me so deeply, but I hated that my grief was doing the same to him.

Millie's voice cut through the thick silence that blanketed the group. "Violet's right." All eyes turned her way. "Sherry and I stayed until everyone else had gone. The man she was with, and the minister practically carried Rhonda to the limo. She was doubled over with grief, even without an audience to play to."

"Are we in agreement then?" Bea asked. "The widow is off the suspect list?"

We all agreed, though Earl reserved the right to change his

mind. Without a solid alibi, Rhonda would remain on his list.

Bea threw out the million-dollar question. "Who else is on the list?"

Everyone looked at everyone else.

"There's got to be someone," I pleaded. "I can't go to jail for something I didn't do!"

"Well," Sherry said, "what about the charities he donated to? I overheard the lady who runs the youth center in town complaining that he'd cut his donation in half this year. If she thought he'd mentioned the center in his will, maybe she offed him for the funds?"

She ended her rambling statement like a question. I could tell she didn't believe her theory any more than we did.

Bea was never one to mince words. "That seems a bit far-fetched, don't you think?"

"Well, I don't hear any of you coming up with anything." Bea's criticism had prickled Sherry's feathers. She sat back in her chair, arms crossed over her middle as she stared at the dancing flames in the pit.

"Did anyone find out if there is a will?" I asked.

Camille darted a questioning gaze toward Earl. His subtle nod encouraged her to speak up. "After we dropped you off this afternoon, we went back into town. To the wake."

"That took balls." I ignored Mason's comment, but he wasn't wrong.

"Oh, my. How did that go?"

"As you said, Rhonda was mired in grief. Sobbing at times. Then she'd buck it up and try to talk to people who stopped by where she was sitting, but as soon as they said something, she'd break down again. It was horrible to watch."

My heart went out to the woman, but my life was on the line here. I had to know. "So? Did you find out if there's a will?"

"There is." Once again, she looked to Earl for guidance. Receiving another head nod from him, she continued. "Ned's lawyer approached me. He said I should be there for the reading."

Everyone gasped at once. Willa recovered first. "Does that mean you're mentioned in the will?"

"I think so." Camille seemed less than pleased about the situation. "The reading is day after tomorrow at three p.m. at the Haggerty Estate."

Kendra asked the question on all our minds. "What's the Haggerty Estate?"

"That's what I said when the attorney mentioned it." Camille sipped wine from the plastic cup she'd been holding. "Have you seen that giant house on the edge of town? The one that looks like a museum or something?" We all nodded.

"The one with the big iron gates and stone lions on the pillars?" Millie inquired.

Camille nodded. "That's the house Ned grew up in. It's now the headquarters for Haggerty Holdings. The house is being used as an office building, and a caretaker lives in the pool house."

Bea whistled low. "Damn. That place alone must be worth a fortune. How much money did Ned have?"

"I have no idea. The attorney said Ned got a monthly allowance from a trust, but that even with Rhonda's elaborate spending on clothes and shoes, most of it was never touched."

Millie chimed in. "She has an enviable wardrobe that must have cost a small fortune."

Rhonda's spending habits were interesting, but not helpful as far as I was concerned. "Did the attorney say who else would be at the reading?"

Earl cleared his throat. "I asked the same question. He named a long list of people, saying they represented various local charities. It sounds like there's going to be a crowd."

Still stuck on the location for the reading, I mused, "Haggerty Holdings. Where have I heard that name before?"

"Is there a sign at the estate? Maybe you saw it when you passed by?"

"I don't know, Sherry. You're partially right, though. I think it was on a sign, just not at the estate."

"You saw it on that flyer taped to the post outside the coffee shop you went to the other day when you were in town for groceries." At the sound of Mason's voice, I snapped my head around to see him leaning casually against Bea's trailer. I narrowed my eyes at him, trying to envision the flyer in question. "It was something about a meeting to discuss new zoning regulations for a piece of land owned by Haggerty Holdings."

"That's it!" I exclaimed, nearly jumping out of my chair. Bud, who'd been sleeping at my feet, sat up and barked. "Sorry about that." I pet him on the head. "Didn't mean to alarm you." I fished a treat out of my pocket for him, and he lay back down to eat it. "As I was about to say, there's a flyer in town notifying residents about a zoning change meeting. Haggerty Holdings wants to rezone a piece of property they own."

"What property?" Bea asked.

I shrugged. "No idea. I didn't read it that closely." Satisfied that I'd remembered where I'd seen the business mentioned, I sat back in my chair and enjoyed a sip of wine.

Sherry reached for a chip and dunked it in a bowl of ranch dip before popping it in her mouth. She talked as she chewed. "Do you think the zoning request could have something to do with Ned's murder?"

"How could it? Ned wasn't involved in the company's day-to-day operations. Was he?"

Murmurs of "I don't know" filled the air as we all contemplated Willa's question.

"It's something we should look into." Earl stood up and stretched in the way only a man does—unselfconsciously. "I'll see what I can find out tomorrow. Zoning rights can be a hot-button issue for lots of people." He held out his hand to his wife. Camille put her hand in his and let him tug her to her feet. "Come on, baby. Let's get some shut-eye."

We watched the young couple stroll across the road and down a few spaces to their borrowed trailer.

"They remind me of us when we were first married." Mason still leaned against Bea's trailer, but he'd rolled so one shoulder supported him. His gaze followed Earl and Camille. I couldn't say anything out loud in front of the others, but when Mason glanced my way, I gave a subtle head nod, agreeing with his observation.

"It is getting late." I made a show of checking the time on my phone. "I've got a lot to do tomorrow."

One by one, we stood and helped Bea clean up before calling it a night. Bud, sensing our night had come to an end, stretched and then ambled toward our trailer. He stopped to take a whiz on the barbecue grill post. I bent to fold my camp chair. Bea stopped me with a hand on my shoulder. Attending Ned's funeral had taken an emotional toll on me, and I was near tears when the older woman engulfed me in a big hug. "You go on now and get a good night's sleep. It's going to be alright, Violet. We'll find out who killed Ned. We'll know more after Earl checks out that zoning thing, and the will is read. I bet we'll have more suspects than we can shake a stick at. Mark my words." With a sharp pat on my back, she set me free. She disappeared into her trailer and closed the door before I could find the words to thank her.

CHAPTER EIGHTEEN

If firing up a 470-horsepower diesel engine in a quiet campground at dawn can be considered sneaking, then I snuck out before I got sucked into another meeting of the Hitchin' the Road Ladies. There was coffee in my cabinet, but I'd spent hours the previous night trying to remember every word I'd read on the zoning meeting flyer and come up short. The only way to rectify that was to take another look at it. And while I was at the coffee shop, I would also enjoy its free Wi-Fi. If the zoning change request were the least bit controversial, it would be the subject of an online discussion.

The flyer confirmed my suspicion that not everyone in town was in favor of the zoning change. The glass garage door that made up the front of the shop was open, allowing patrons to sit in or out as they pleased. I claimed a table for myself and Bud in the center of the outdoor seating area, where I could eavesdrop on several conversations at once. There was just enough room on the tabletop for my open laptop, a coffee cup, and a plate containing a chocolate croissant that had called my name. The latte was as good as I remembered from the other day, and the croissant tasted like it had been crafted by angels. I took a moment to savor both before searching the internet for local gossip groups. As expected, there were several, only one of which I could access without answering questions about my residency and interests. I clicked into the group feed, found the little magnifying glass Elle had shown me how to use, and searched the group for any mention of zoning changes. I sat back, wide-eyed as dozens of posts popped up. After a few seconds of scrolling, I hit the jackpot. One post had hundreds of comments about the proposed new data center a major online retailer supposedly wanted to build nearby. Angry words were exchanged on both sides of the issue, and as far as I could tell, both sides made good points. At the center of the controversy was a parcel of land owned by Haggerty Holdings.

"Find anything interesting?"

The sound of Detective Donaldson's voice startled me into nearly knocking my laptop off the table. He and I reached for it at the same time, our hands brushing momentarily in the process. There might have been a zing of electricity when we touched, but then again, it was more likely a case of nerves on my part. There had been no zing when he slapped handcuffs on me.

"That's because he was arresting you for murder, Vi. I bet if he cuffed you to a bed, you'd feel the zing."

Mason had always had an uncanny way of reading my mind, but you know what they say about losing one of your senses. It heightens your other senses. He'd lost nearly all his senses, touch, taste, smell, but the loss seemed to have enhanced his ability to read my mind. Since I couldn't express my exasperation with my husband's ghost in a public place, and especially not in front of the detective who had arrested me, I settled for glaring at the very human person who'd taken the seat opposite me. "Are you here to arrest me for using the free Wi-Fi for too long? Or maybe for the sin of drinking a latte too slow?"

The man really was too handsome for his own good when he smiled. I resisted the urge to kick him under the table. Barely.

"It was my turn to bring coffee for the office crew," he said, by way of explanation. Bud sat on his haunches and pawed at the interloper, begging for attention. Donaldson extended his hand. "Shake?" Much to my surprise, Bud put his paw in the detective's hand. "Good boy!" the detective praised. He tore off a bite of my croissant (just the bread part, no chocolate) and held it out for Bud. Darn the man for weaseling his way into my dog's good graces, and double darn for knowing not to give chocolate to a dog. He gave Bud some sort of hand signal, and the canine plopped to the floor, his snout resting on his front paws. What was this? Some sort of dog sorcery?

Donaldson's voice snapped my attention away from my suddenly compliant dog. "Anyway, some of the orders are complicated." He hitched a thumb over his shoulder to indicate the barista visible through the open door. "Weather permitting, I sit out here while I wait for Bailey to do her magic." His gaze dropped to my laptop. "What are you doing up so early?"

"I'm an early riser by nature," I lied. Mason had been the one to rise before the sun, while I preferred to wake whenever my body was ready. That had never been this early until I took to the road. The Airstream was nice, but I heard every bird chirp, and smelled every breakfast cooking over an open fire. "Besides, I was out of coffee." I don't know why I felt the need to lie to this man, but I'd done it twice in less than a minute.

His gaze held mine for a heartbeat longer than necessary. He knew I was making things up as I went along. My cheeks heated. Damnit! I was blushing like a schoolgirl. Donaldson smirked. The barista called his name. Without taking his eyes off me, he called out, "Thanks, Bailey. I'll be right there." He pointed a finger at me. "Nice try, Violet, but I can see right through you." With a last pat on the head for Bud, the man picked up his order and left without a backward glance.

"You should give him a chance, Vi."

The place was nearly empty, and the closest customers were several tables away from me. I ducked my head, hoping the laptop screen would shield my lips from anyone who might see me talking to myself. Knowing Mason would hear me, I mumbled, "Don't go there, Mason. I'm not ready. I don't know if I ever will be." I tapped a few keys to make it look like I was working in earnest.

"I'd like to see you settled before I go."

That did it. I slapped my computer shut, shoved it into the oversized tote I kept it in, and stormed toward the door. Heads raised as I passed by, so I slowed until I was on the sidewalk. I made it to the truck without exploding. Backed away from the curbside parking spot without exploding. Made it through the town's single traffic light without exploding. But as soon as I hit the open road, I let Mason have it. "Don't you ever talk to me like that again! You're the love of my life, Mason. There will never be anyone else like you. So, if that's why you're still here, then you can just jolly well be on your way." I spied what looked like a turnout and pulled the truck off the road. I slammed the gearshift into Park seconds before the waterworks began.

"I'm sorry, Vi."

"Will you quit saying you're sorry? I know you didn't leave me on purpose, despite what Kurt said. And I know you want me to move on, but I can't, Mason. I don't want to. Maybe one day, but not now. Not when I see you and talk to you every day. I see more of you now than I did when you were alive."

"I'm—"

The look on my face stopped him before he could say it again. The crunch of gravel beneath tires had me glancing in the rearview mirror. "Darn it. Can't the man take a hint?" Getting out of his department-issued sedan was none other than Ray Donaldson.

As he approached, I rolled down my window. Bud, tail wagging, the traitor, tried to climb into my lap. "Are you following me, Detective?"

"Nope. I'm on my way to ask a witness in another case a few more questions. I saw your vehicle off the road and thought I'd stop to make sure you're okay." He eyed me like he knew I wasn't okay.

"I'm having a bad day." Not a lie. "I stopped to take in the view." I swept my hand toward the passenger-side window, where there was a magnificent view of the valley below. If I were in a better mood, I'd take time to appreciate it more. Bud took advantage of my distraction and barreled into my lap and stuck his nose out the window.

"Hey there, Bud." He scratched the mutt behind his ears. "This is some watchdog you have here."

"Bud! Get back!" Bud slammed into my face as he tried to turn around in my lap rather than back out gracefully. His backside pressed into the horn, the sharp sound startling both him and me. He bounded into the backseat like his tail was on fire. "Ugh." Wiping dog hair from my lips, I powered down the backseat window—something I should have done to begin with—and my clumsy canine stuck his head out for more ear rubs. Donaldson complied, though his amused gaze remained fixed on me. I fought the urge to squirm.

"I hope your day gets better." His smirk said he knew just how much his presence bothered me. "But, in case it doesn't…" He pulled a business card out of his wallet and, reaching in the window, placed it on my dashboard. "If I can be of any help, Violet, call me. Day or night."

For the second time that morning, the man walked away

without a backward glance. I know, because I watched him in the side-view mirror. If I were in the market for a man, he'd be just the type I'd be interested in.

"He reminds me of me."

"Shut up, Mason."

CHAPTER NINETEEN

I bypassed the turnoff for the campground and continued until I came upon a sign announcing the local Renaissance Faire. The parking lot was empty at this time of day, as I expected. I wasn't there to take part in the festivities. According to my research, this was the parcel of land Haggerty Holdings had requested a zoning change for. A plethora of yard signs, some professionally printed, others handwritten, lined the parking lot and entrance to the event. Notices for the zoning board meeting decorated the rustic ticket booth along with handmade signs pleading with fair-goers to attend the meeting and make their objections known.

There was no one around to tell me I couldn't enter, so, Bud at my side, I wandered into the medieval village. Period-appropriate signage directed me to go left for the jousting arena, right for the village shoppes, and straight ahead to be heard before the royal court. Since all I was interested in was the land itself, we went left, figuring the open arena would be my best bet to avoid people. I was wrong. The arena was a beehive of activity. Being a city girl, I hadn't considered that the horses would need to be fed and exercised. Several of the magnificent animals paraded around the open-air arena. Without riders to dictate their behavior, they frolicked like children at recess. I leaned against the rail. Bud seemed as transfixed as I was by their beauty and antics.

"They're something to see, aren't they?"

I'd been so wrapped up in watching the horses, I hadn't noticed the woman who'd joined me at the rail. Dressed in dusty jeans and a long-sleeved plaid shirt, and wearing a wide-brimmed cowboy hat and well-worn boots, she could have been from another century. Despite her weathered complexion, the cellphone clutched in her hand placed her firmly in the 21st century. "Yes," I replied. "They're magnificent." I didn't even try to hide the awe in my voice.

"The Faire doesn't open for a few more hours."

Her chastisement was nonconfrontational. "I know. I didn't come for the entertainment. I just wanted to get a look at the land."

"Why?" Her hard stare and harder question were as confrontational as they could be.

I shrugged. "I don't know, exactly. I'm camping nearby and heard about the zoning hearing in town, and thought I'd take a look. See what all the fuss is about."

"You aren't a local resident, or worse, a developer?"

"No. I'm at the campground for a few more weeks. It's not a bad place to camp, but if they build a data center on this property…" I let the thought trail off. As she said, I'm not a resident. There's nothing I can do except maybe voice my opinion at the zoning meeting, if they let non-residents speak.

"If they succeed in rezoning the property, the Faire and the campground probably won't be here next year."

"What do you mean? I thought this piece of property was the only one up for rezoning."

"It is, but we're talking about over a thousand acres. The Ren Faire occupies about six acres. The campground is about twice that. That's eighteen acres out of a thousand. The rest is pristine forest that's home to dozens of varieties of wildlife that would have no place to go. Not to mention the hiking trails people come from all over to enjoy. It would all be gone. Bulldozed and paved over so some conglomerate can speed up the response time on their website. Not to mention the drain on our power grid and our water supply. It takes a lot of both to keep those computers running."

"You sound very knowledgeable on the subject."

"I've lived here all my life, and I pay attention. Haggerty Holdings has no conscience."

"What about Ned Haggerty? Where did he stand on the zoning issue?"

"God rest his soul. Ned was the only person on the Haggerty Holding board with any sense. Now that he's gone, his wife will probably sell all his properties to big tech companies."

"All his properties?"

"Haggerty Holdings owns twenty-five percent of the land in this county."

I made a low whistling sound. "That much?"

She nodded. "And most of it is undeveloped. Ned insisted on keeping it that way. Now that he's gone, there's nothing to stop Rhonda from selling it all."

"Except the zoning issues," I surmised.

A heavy sigh accompanied her next words. "You know who the zoning commissioner is, don't you?"

"No. Who?"

"Calvin Dreyer. Rhonda's cousin. His dad's the Chief of Police."

"Oh." Silence fell between us as I let this new information marinate in my brain. Besides inheriting an already robust estate, Rhonda Haggerty stood to make a fortune by selling off the land included in the estate. And if what I suspected was true, she'd have no problem pushing through the zoning changes needed to make the land attractive to big tech conglomerates. Just to clarify, I asked, "How did Ned and Calvin get along?"

"They hated each other. Ned went to every public zoning meeting and made his objections known. He'd invariably sway enough members to his way of thinking, so when it came time to vote on the change, Calvin and his cronies would lose. It's because of Ned that this town doesn't have a host of megastores lining the main drag."

"Calvin and his cronies?"

"They're mostly real estate agents, developers, and representatives of the largest single landowner in the county."

"Haggerty Holdings."

"You catch on quick."

Wranglers came out to round up the horses, and my time there was coming to a close.

I held my hand out. "Violet Hartwell, camper," I said in a let's be friends voice.

She extended her hand, and we shook. "Beverly Carson, legal secretary. Before you ask, I've always loved horses, but I can't afford to own one, so I'm a volunteer groomer here on my days off."

"That must be satisfying work."

"It is. The horses are awesome, and the stable hands appreciate the help."

As we strolled back toward the front gate, I asked, "How well did you know Ned?"

Beverly laughed. "We went to school together, like every other kid in this town. We went to Senior Prom together."

"Wow! I guess you knew him pretty well then."

We'd made it to the gate. Beverly leaned against the building like she wasn't in any hurry to leave. "We were good together for a while. Then we weren't. You know how high school romances go."

"What happened?"

"We both went our separate ways for college, and when we came back, we were different people. That's all there is to it."

"Did you try to make it work?"

She shook her head. "Nah. Too much water under the bridge, and all that. He was at odds with his dad, and fighting that fight took all his energy."

"Sounds like you might still have had a thing for him."

"Wouldn't have mattered if I did. Rhonda got her hooks into him. Thought she could change him, or maybe she just wanted his money."

I thought about Rhonda's abject grief I'd witnessed at the cemetery. "Did you go to the funeral?"

"No. I said goodbye to him long ago."

If anyone knew grief, it was me. Ned's death weighed heavily on Beverly Carson, whether or not she admitted it. A thought occurred to me. "Did you ever marry? Have children?"

She narrowed her eyes at me. "No. Never married. No children. Why would you ask that?"

I shrugged. "Just curious." I urged Bud to his feet. "Well, I'd better get going. It was nice meeting you, and thanks for bringing me up to speed on the local politics."

"You're welcome."

Mason had been quiet throughout my conversation with Beverly, but as soon as I turned onto the main road, headed toward the campground, he materialized in the passenger seat.

"You need to attend the zoning meeting tonight."

CHAPTER TWENTY

"I think you might be right." The fuel gauge read a quarter of a tank, so I pulled into the filling station at the corner of the main highway and the road to the campground. The big vehicle guzzled diesel on its own. Add the Airstream to the mix, and I had to keep a close eye on the tank, or I'd find myself stranded in unfamiliar territory. I cut the engine and dug into my purse for my wallet and the credit card Mason had opened specifically for fuel purchases. It was one of those where you earned airline points for every dollar spent, and you got double points at gas stations. We were going to save up and use the points for tickets to Ireland. A second honeymoon, which was ironic since we'd never had a first one.

Closing my eyes, I clutched the card in my hand and forced the memories away. There'd be no trip to Ireland, points or no points. I had no desire to make the trip alone. As usual, Mason seemed to have read my mind. "I'm sorry, Violet. I was really looking forward to taking you to Ireland."

"I know. I was looking forward to going." With a sigh, I opened the door and dropped to the pavement. After filling the tank, I climbed behind the wheel again and tucked the card away in my wallet. "Maybe I can use the points for something else. Or gift them to the kids."

"You'll go to Ireland, like we planned." Mason was a hard man to budge when he had his mind set.

"Can we *not* talk about Ireland? Besides, if I don't figure out who killed Ned, the only place I'll be going is to prison. No points necessary for that trip."

"You're going to Ireland." His tone of voice told me he was through discussing the subject, which was fine by me. "And you aren't going to prison. Beverly Carson was a fountain of information. I can think of half a dozen people who had more reason to murder Ned than you."

"Everyone has more reason to murder him than I do. I didn't even know him."

"And most of them will be at the zoning meeting tonight."

"Yeah. I figured that out on my own." I backed the truck into my parking spot and cut the engine.

***

It seemed like everyone in town had turned out for the hearing, and the list of people requesting to have their say was as long as my arm, so I didn't bother to add my name to the list. I found a place to stand along the back wall and listened as Calvin Dreyer introduced the zoning board members seated on the small stage. Once the formalities were out of the way, he introduced Paul Everett, the Chairman of the Board of Haggerty Holdings, who expounded on the virtues of the proposed data center. It was all bullshit, and everyone in the audience knew it, and they said as much, often at the top of their lungs. I felt somewhat sorry for Mr. Everett, as he was almost heckled off the stage several times. Every time the crowd grew too rowdy, Calvin would rap his gavel on the table and threaten to have them all removed from the building. His father, the police chief, and several uniformed officers stood near the stage, adding credence to the commissioner's threat.

Feeling claustrophobic, I was about to leave when a gray-haired lady stood up, and shaking her frail fist at Mr. Everett, shouted out, "I should box your ears, Paulie, for all the lies you're spouting up there. Your mother, God rest her sainted soul, would be ashamed of you!"

"This is finally getting interesting." Mason wasn't wrong. Up until then, the meeting had been lively but predictable.

Shouts of support from the already enraged crowd fueled the woman's tirade. "You were always looking for a way to make another buck, but this is beyond the pale, Paulie. Everyone in this town knows you and your board don't give a flying fig about this town." She turned her attention to Calvin Dreyer. "And you, you little prick! You were a bully when you were a teenager, and you're an even bigger bully now. Instead of stealing lunch money from little kids, now you're taking kickbacks from big tech companies to push the zoning changes through. When the two of you are done, there won't be anything left of our town. The roads will be lined with concrete boxes, and your pockets will be lined with cash." She pointed a bony finger at the stage. "Which one of you murdered Ned? Huh? One of you did, because he was the only person standing between you and the money."

A collective gasp rose from the audience. Time stood still for a heartbeat, then all hell broke loose. The audience seemed to move as one, shouting and advancing toward the stage. Calvin called for order, to no avail, as the officers tried to prevent nimble residents from jumping onto the stage.

"Time to go." Mason didn't have to tell me twice. Luckily, I'd chosen a space near an emergency exit. A few steps brought me to the door. I leaned against the release bar. Sirens blared as I pushed the door open and made my escape.

Halfway down the block, I stopped to catch my breath. "What just happened?"

"That was a mutiny," Mason declared.

"I wonder who that lady was. She certainly stirred up a hornet's nest."

"She seemed to know Dreyer and Everett pretty well."

People were streaming out of the building, heading off in every direction. A few came my way. I recognized the woman I'd spoken to at the Ren Faire earlier. "Hi, Beverly." I stepped forward so she could see my face under the streetlamp. "Remember me? We met at the arena?"

She looked me over. Recognition dawned, but she didn't stop walking. "Violet! I'm surprised to see you here," she said, confirming that she remembered me. I fell into step beside her.

"It sounded like a good time, and it didn't disappoint." Her legs were a lot longer than mine, and I was nearly breathless trying to keep up. "Who was that lady? The one that caused the riot?"

"That was Miss Abigail Stump. She taught high school English to everyone who ever went through the local school system for the last forty years. She's a local institution."

Mason chimed in. "Well, that explains how she knows both men."

"Do you think there's any truth in her accusations? Could one of those men have murdered Ned?"

My companion stopped at an intersection, and after looking at the deserted streets, crossed against the light. I'd never ignored a don't walk signal in my life, but tamping down my do-gooder instincts, I kept pace with her. When we reached the other side, she spoke. "The reason Paul Everett is so scrawny is probably because Calvin stole his lunch money every day for years. Paul never had the guts to stand up to Calvin, and his wife runs roughshod over him now. Controlling the board of Haggarty Holdings is his way of compensating for not having any balls. Would he kill Ned to get what he wants? No."

She stopped beside an older model sedan in dire need of a wash. She pushed a button on a key fob. The lights flashed, and the door locks disengaged. "I can't say the same about Calvin Dreyer. He'd kill his own grandmother to shut her up." I was still standing on the sidewalk, contemplating her comments, when she rolled the window down and dropped a verbal bomb on me. "Miss Stump better watch her back."

"Wait. What?"

"Abigail Stump is Calvin Dreyer's grandmother on his mother's side."

CHAPTER TWENTY-ONE

"Close your mouth, Vi. You'll catch a June Bug."

My jaw seemed to have come unhinged. Snapping my mouth shut, I refused to acknowledge Mason's comment. Instead, I crossed the street to where I'd left my truck. Bud was home alone. I needed to get back to let him out to do his business.

"Well, that was certainly interesting."

"That Paul Everett has no balls, or that Calvin Dreyer's grandmother just publicly humiliated him?" There were people everywhere, making my progress out of town treacherous. I'd already been accused of murder. Running someone over wouldn't help my cause.

"I'm glad you haven't lost your sense of humor, Vi." Mason's laugh sent a spear of longing through my heart. I don't know which was harder, accepting that he was gone for good, or having this spectral reminder of all I'd lost prodding at my grief when I least expected it. "Pedestrian at two o'clock."

I hit the brakes just as an old woman waving a cane in the air stepped off the curb into the glare of my headlights. "What the—" I leaned over the steering wheel, narrowing my eyes to get a better look. I'd previously only seen the woman from the back. "Is that...?

"Abigail Stump." Mason answered my question before I could ask it. "Better see what she wants."

Bounding out of the truck, which was still in the middle of the traffic lane, I moved into the glare of the headlights. "Miss Stump? What are you doing?"

"I'm flagging you down. What does it look like?" She leaned on her cane. "We need to talk."

"Ooookay." Another car was approaching. We needed to get out of there, and quick. "Can I give you a lift home?"

"Not my place. I'm not safe there. Take me to your place."

Despite the cane, the woman moved fast. Before I knew it, she was hoisting herself up into the passenger seat of my truck. I hustled around the vehicle and settled behind the wheel. I pressed the accelerator with a heavy foot.

"Guess you really are one of the campers." Miss Stump craned her neck, checking out the campground from the dark cab of my pickup. "Makes sense they'd try to pin Ned's murder on a transient."

Being called *transient* made me wince. My plan was to be on my way in a few weeks, and despite the word's negative connotation, it fit. The irony was, this woman might be the key to my being able to leave of my own free will. "Why do you say that, Miss Stump?"

"Call me Abby. I always hated the name Stump, but I loved Rupert, God rest his soul, and if I wanted him, I had to take the name too."

Guessing her to be close to eighty, I suppose she'd had no choice but to take her husband's last name back then. "Abby," I corrected. "Who do you think is trying to pin Ned's murder on me, and why would they do that?"

"You were at the meeting tonight. I saw you, so don't deny it. You heard me plain enough. One of *them* did it. My money's on that no-good Calvin Dreyer. He's meaner than Scratch. Always has been. As to why, well, isn't that obvious? It's easier to blame someone we don't know than it is to accept that one of our own is a cold-blooded murderer. No one wants to believe that."

"But you do?"

"Well, I know it wasn't you. I've done some checking. You'd only been here a few hours before you found poor Ned's body. Unless you were hired to kill him, then what motive would you have?" She quirked an eyebrow at me. "You aren't a hired killer, are you?"

"No. I'm not."

Both bony hands wrapped around the crooked handle of her cane, she thumped the floorboard twice. "There you have it. You didn't do it. But somebody did. Poor Ned didn't stab himself."

"What about Paul Everett? Or one of the other members of the Haggerty Holdings board of directors?"

The old woman pursed her lips, giving the idea some thought. "Like I said, Paul hasn't got any balls. Never had any. He let Calvin walk all over him in school, and his wife, Natalie, has been telling him what color underwear to put on since the day she told him to marry her." Abby shook a claw-like finger at me. "He didn't get along with Ned. I think he always resented him because Ned had all that money, and he didn't even want it, while Paul's momma barely scraped together lunch money for him, which made it all the more inconceivable that he let Calvin take it away from him. You'd have thought he'd have had more respect for what his ma did for him." Hands resting on the handle of her cane, she gazed out the truck window. "You got anything to drink in that fancy trailer of yours?"

"How about some coffee?"

"I was thinking about something a little stronger."

"Wine?"

"That'll have to do, I guess." She popped the truck door open and slid off the seat. When her feet hit the ground, all I could see was the top of her gray head. I popped open my door and met her underneath the awning. "Who's that?" she asked.

"That's Bea." I waved at my neighbor. "Come on. I'll introduce you."

We made our way over, and as I suspected, Bea and Abby hit it off immediately. I excused myself to find the wine I'd promised. When I returned with Bud and plastic wine glasses for myself and Abby, and two bottles of wine, the rest of my newfound friends had arrived. I filled everyone in on what transpired at the meeting, then turned to Abby. "You were about to tell me why you think Calvin might have murdered Ned."

The old woman nodded. "Yep. I was." Glancing at the women gathered around the firepit, she dove right into the story. "Like I told Violet, both Paul and Calvin had reason to want Ned out of the way, but Paul's balls never dropped, so I can't seriously believe he'd murder anyone. That leaves Calvin. He popped out of the womb with a nasty attitude, and it only got worse with age. Ned might be the only person to ever call Calvin on his shit. When Calvin demanded Paul hand over his lunch money, the sniveling coward handed it over along with the lint from the bottom of his pocket. Ned, not so much." She looked off into the distance, a smile gracing her wrinkled face as she recalled long-ago days. "I overheard them one day as I was heading to my classroom. Calvin had Ned cornered next to a bank of lockers. I didn't hear Calvin's demands, but I heard Ned clear as a bell. 'You can't have my lunch money, Cal, but if you're short of funds, I'll loan you enough to buy lunch.' I stopped in my tracks, waiting to hear Calvin's response."

We were on the edge of our seats. "What did Calvin do?" I asked.

"He was livid," she recalled. "Told Ned where he could shove his loan, if you know what I mean. I heard a loud *oof.* Assumed Calvin had punched Ned in the gut, and I wasn't wrong. Calvin turned his back on Ned. Then Ned…" Abby cackled and slapped a hand against her leg as tears streamed down her cheeks. She tried again. "Then I heard Ned, cool as a cucumber, say, 'I shit bigger turds than you, Dreyer.'"

"Wow. That took some guts." Millie topped off Abby's wine as the older woman wiped the moisture from her cheeks.

Abby nodded. "Damn right it did. The thing is, Ned would have given Calvin money if he'd asked nicely."

"What about Paul? He really needed money. Did Ned offer him any?"

The old woman shook her head. "Nah. Don't reckon Paul would have taken it if Ned had offered." She sighed into her wine. "Not many people knew it, but the lunch ladies felt sorry for Paul, so they let him eat for free most days. At least, that's what everyone thought. I found out years later from Ruby, who worked the cafeteria cash register at the time, that Ned paid for his and Paul's lunch every single day. He never said a word about it. Never asked for any recognition. Just handed Ruby twice what his lunch cost."

"Where did Paul think the money came from?"

"That first day he did it, Ned told Ruby to tell Paul his momma thought he was spending his lunch money on candy at the 7-11 on the way home from school, so she came in and paid for the entire year upfront. As far as I know, Paul never caught on that Ned was his benefactor."

"It would be plain awful if Paul was the one who killed Ned."

Bea had the right of it.

"Like I said. Paul didn't do it. He might be a rat in his business dealings, but he was a mouse as a kid. And a spineless one at that." Abby shook her head. It was clear no one was going to change her mind on the subject. She fixed her gaze on Camille. "What have you got to say for yourself, young lady? I hear tell you're Ned's daughter. Did you murder him for the inheritance?"

Camille's spine straightened. She looked the newcomer in the eye. "No. I hardly knew the man, and I didn't know he had any more than two nickels to rub together. I doubt I'm entitled to anything or that I'd take it if it were handed to me. I have plenty of money of my own."

Before Abby could question the younger woman's statement, I jumped in. "Camille's job pays well." I explained that it was Ned's idea for her and Earl to stay in the crappy rental. "She was just trying to get to know her biological father."

"Well, if Violet vouches for you, then I guess I'll take you off my list of suspects."

"We heard Ned was a womanizer and that he may have cheated on his wife. Do you know anything about that?" Sherry asked.

Abby nodded toward Camille. "Don't get me wrong, missy. Deep down, Ned was a good kid, and a good man, for the most part. I don't know what happened, but when he came home from college, he was different. He'd become a terrible flirt."

"He wasn't like that in high school?" I queried.

"No ma'am. He dated, like all young men did, but his senior year, he was stuck on one girl."

"Beverly Carson?" I asked.

Abby raised both eyebrows. "You know Beverly?"

"Not really," I answered. "I met her this morning at the Faire grounds. She told me s he and Ned went to Senior Prom together."

"That's right. They did." Abby stared into the fire for a second or two, then she glanced at Camille, then back at me. "Did she say what happened after that? I always thought they would get married after graduation."

"All she said was that after prom, they went their separate ways. Then when they returned from college, they were different people."

"She wasn't wrong about that. After college, Ned came on to

every woman he met, and from what I hear, bedded more than his share. Before and after he and Rhonda said I do. To my knowledge, he and Beverly never had anything to do with one another after that."

Bea got up and dropped another log onto the fire. "Seems like that kind of behavior would result in a lot of irate husbands and boyfriends. Maybe one of them killed him."

"That's a possibility," Abby conceded.

It was good to have our assumption about Ned's affairs confirmed, but adding countless names to the suspect list didn't bode well for me. "I wish we knew who his latest conquest was. Ned's murder was brutal—a crime of passion, which leads me to believe the killer's grievance was recent. Passions dull over time."

"I know you don't think Rhonda did it, but what if she finally had had enough and snapped?"

Bea shook her head. "Nope. Wasn't Rhonda. I wandered over to the other side of the campground today while I was waiting for my laundry to spin. Talked to the family that checked in right after Violet did. There was some snafu with their reservations, and it took Rhonda a while to sort it all out. She was there the whole time. Never left their sight. The woman said Rhonda was mighty pissed that Ned wasn't there to help. Kept calling him on that walkie-talkie thing he carries around, but he didn't answer."

"I remember them." I reached down and rubbed Bud on the head. "Husband and wife? Three kids, if I recall? They had one of those fancy bus-sized campers and were towing a Jeep."

"That's them," Bea confirmed. "And since you saw Ned alive when you checked in, and they were there until the police arrived, that means Rhonda couldn't have done it."

"There goes one of your prime suspects." I closed my eyes and shook my head at Mason's unnecessary comment. I'd already decided that Rhonda hadn't killed Ned.

"So where do I go from here?" I threw the question out into the universe. "The wife didn't do it. Ned's nemesis at his own company didn't do it. However, we have an endless list of cuckolded husbands and boyfriends, and locals who didn't like Ned's stance on land preservation." With a glance at Camille, I silently added drug dealers to my list. Mentioning that would out Earl and possibly derail his investigation. There was the possibility that Ned was involved in drug trafficking, or that he'd stumbled upon it and was murdered to guarantee his silence.

Not that I expected them to, but no one chimed in with a viable candidate to fill the role of murderer. There were just too many actors to choose from, which made my situation seem hopeless.

"Don't worry, Vi. We'll get you out of this mess." I mentally noted that for once, Mason hadn't said we'd locate the real killer.

"Orange isn't my color." I glanced around the fire pit at my new friends. "I have to clear my name, and fast."

CHAPTER TWENTY-TWO

Abby figured tempers had cooled enough that it was safe to go home. Just to make sure, I swallowed my pride and called Detective Donaldson's private line. He answered on the first ring.

"Violet. Is everything okay?"

"How did you know it was me?"

A warm chuckle filled the line. "I hoped you would call me, so I put your number in my phone."

I let that realization sink in for a moment, then I got down to the reason I had called him. "I guess you heard about what happened at the zoning meeting tonight?"

"I did. How do you know about it?"

"I was there."

"Why in the world would you go to that?"

"I went because it's possible Ned was murdered because of his opposition to the zoning change." Ignoring Donaldson's groan, I continued. "Anyway, Abigail Stump came home with me. I'm going to take her home now, but I was wondering if you could arrange for someone to keep tabs on her house tonight? Just to make sure she's okay?"

"I'll do better than that," he said. "Stay right where you are. I'll pick Mrs. Stump up and take her home myself. Then I'll call dispatch and request frequent patrols in her neighborhood tonight."

"I can take her home."

"You could, but you won't. Stay put. I'm on my way." The stubborn man hung up before I could tell him what to do with his macho act.

I filled Abby in on the change of plans. "Ray always was a good kid. He was one of the few who read every book I assigned. I heard he did well in college, too."

We took Bud for a walk around our side of the campground and had just returned when Ray Donaldson drove up. His attire of well-worn jeans, a dark t-shirt, and tennis shoes gave off a relaxed vibe, but his expression said otherwise.

"Thanks for coming," I said. "I could have taken Abby home."

Ray's gaze landed briefly on Abby. "Mrs. Stump," he said, before turning his attention back to me. "You don't know how to stay out of trouble, do you?"

The man sure knew how to rile me up. "I've done nothing, and you know it. If the police in this town had a lick of sense, they'd know I didn't murder Ned."

"I know it. And you know it."

"Me, too," Abby said with a huff.

Donaldson nodded at the old woman. "And Mrs. Stump knows it. Since you didn't do it, someone else did, and that someone is still out there. Did it occur to you that if you poke too close to the truth, the killer might come after you next?"

It had occurred to me, but what was I supposed to do? "So, I'm supposed to sit around and wait to be convicted of something I didn't do?" Rage burned hot in my veins. I got right up in the detective's face. "I won't do that. I *can't* do that. My children need me, Detective. I don't care how many bears I have to poke. I'm going to clear my name."

"You hear that, Ray?" Mrs. Stump jabbed her cane at the detective. "I've done all I could. I poked a few bears of my own this evening. My no-good son-in-law isn't going to do a thing, but I expect better of you. So, are you going to help the lady? Or not?"

Throughout Abby's tirade, Ray hadn't taken his eyes off me. I couldn't decide whether he was contemplating strangling me or kissing me. It could have been either or both. Finally, he took a step back, breaking eye contact and severing the strange connection that had formed between us. "I'm thinking about it." He waved a hand at Abby. "Come on, Mrs. Stump. I'll get you home."

Ever the gentleman, he opened the passenger side door for her before climbing behind the wheel. Bud barked at the bright headlights as the car backed onto the road. I patted Bud on the head. He hadn't growled once at the detective but had remained by my side the whole time. "Good boy. You deserve a treat, don't you think?"

"He's going to be too big to fit through the door if you keep giving him treats for every little thing."

"Mind your own business, Mason."

"You are my business, Vi. And from the looks that detective was giving you, you're his business, too."

I washed the plastic wine glasses I'd put in the sink earlier and set them aside to dry. "Don't be ridiculous. I'm a pain in his side. That's all."

"He's the kind of man you need, Vi."

I could count the times that I'd been raging mad at my husband on one hand and still have a finger left to salute him with. The last time he'd caused my blood to boil was the day he drove off that road and ruined everything. Slapping the dish towel down on the countertop, I turned on him. "I don't need a man, Mason. I had one, and he did the unforgivable. He left me without giving me a chance to say goodbye. I'll be damned if I let another one cause me that kind of pain."

"Violet..."

Pounding on the door, followed by Bud barking his head off, cut off Mason's reply. Wiping tears from my eyes, I called out, "Who's there?"

"Violet? It's me, Bea. Are you okay? I heard a lot of yelling."

Jerking the door open, I put a smile on my face. "Just having a small meltdown. Nothing to worry about. It's just me and Bud."

The older woman stuck her head in the door, and after satisfying herself that I wasn't fending off a murderer in my camper, she nodded. "Okey dokey. You know, if you want to talk, I'll listen. Anytime. Day or night."

"I know," I said with the utmost sincerity. "And thank you. I may take you up on that the next time I feel the need to yell at my dead husband."

"I get it. I truly do." With a warm smile and a wave, she walked back to her camper and closed the door.

I spent a long, lonely night thinking about what my next move should be. Mason wisely stayed away. When I opened the door to let Bud out to do his morning business, Bea, coffee in hand, occupied one of my two lawn chairs. "'bout time you woke up."

Barefoot, and still in my rattiest, and therefore most

comfortable pajamas, I stepped down, arms crossed against the slight chill in the air, and watched Bud sniff around until he found the perfect spot to squat. Thankfully, it was within the confines of my campsite, so the cleanup could wait until I was fully awake. "It was a rough night," I confided. "I didn't sleep well."

"Figured as much." The old woman held up a thermos. "Brought you some coffee. We need to talk."

No need to ask what we needed to talk about. Even if I didn't know, Bea would tell me soon enough. Bud trotted over to examine his food and water bowls. Both were empty. "Let me take care of Bud and put some clothes on." Discussing my imminent incarceration required a more suitable wardrobe. And shoes. Everyone facing a murder rap should have shoes on. I took care of Bud, then myself. When I returned, dressed in white capris and a white sleeveless top adorned with bright purple flowers, Bea was right where I'd left her. I held out Mason's favorite mug for a fill-up. Steam billowed from the fragrant brew. I inhaled the life-giving scent, then touched the rim to my lips. As usual, the liquid was strong enough that she could probably use it as an alternative fuel source if she ran out of gas in the wilderness. It was exactly what I needed. I'd definitely run out of gas.

After a couple of sips of the high-octane brew, I was ready to face my dismal future. "What did you think of Abby Stump?"

Bea rested her mug on the arm of the chair as she gazed off into the distance. "She's got spunk. Did she really accuse her grandson of murder? In front of all those people?"

"She did. I didn't know about their relationship until later, or I probably wouldn't have picked her up and brought her here."

"It's a good thing you did. She made a lot of good points."

"Mmm hmm." I closed my eyes, thinking back over all Abby had revealed. "I think she's right. Paul didn't do it."

"You should still go talk to him. Maybe he knows who did? He and Calvin can't be the only ones who would profit from that data center going in."

Bud ambled over and sat next to my chair, silently begging for a head rub. I obliged. "If Abby's assessment of the man is accurate, then I'd have to agree. Still doesn't mean he didn't hire someone to murder Ned."

Bea shook her head. "Hired killers don't get up close and personal."

"You're right. Multiple stab wounds suggest rage." Silence stretched between us as we downed our coffee and thought more on the subject. Bea broke the spell. "You need to talk to Paul. In person. Take your own measure of the man. Or mouse, as the case may be."

"I hate to admit it, but you're right. It's a weekday. He should be in the office."

I found a pair of slacks and a silk blouse I'd put in the camper on the off-chance Mason and I would have the occasional dinner out somewhere. The outfit leaned more toward 'romantic dinner' than 'interrogate a potential murderer in his office', but it was better than the shorts and capris I normally wear.

"You shouldn't do this alone, Vi." Mason repeated the statement all the way to the gates of the Haggerty Estate, now the corporate headquarters for Haggerty Holdings. "At least call Detective Donaldson and ask him to join you."

"I'm just going in to talk to the man. Get a sense of whether he's capable of murder."

"How are you going to determine that, Vi? Antagonize him until he tries to murder you?"

"Of course not. I've always been an excellent judge of character. If he's as spineless as Abby says he is, then I've nothing to worry about."

"For the record, Vi, this is a bad idea."

The massive home loomed ahead as I navigated the winding driveway. I could see why Ned hadn't wanted to live there. The place gave off a cold vibe, but for the life of me, I couldn't pinpoint where the feeling originated, and I didn't want to admit Mason was right about asking someone to accompany me.

"The place looks haunted."

I hit the brakes so hard that my purse flew off the seat, dumping its contents onto the passenger-side floorboard. "This. From a ghost? Seriously, Mason?" I'd probably never find everything I'd had in my purse. Resigned to having to scavenge for my belongings, I continued up the drive. "It's a good thing I brought you along, then. Ghosts can see other ghosts, can't they?"

"How should I know?"

The driveway led around the house to an enormous six-car garage. Three of the closed garage doors had cars parked in front of them. Visitors' parking signs were attached to the other three. I pulled into the one closest to the house in case I needed to make a quick exit.

Discreet signage directed visitors along a brick walkway to a side entrance. I pressed a button and smiled at the camera on the video doorbell. A moment later, I heard a buzz, and the *snick* of a lock disengaging. Mason stood on the other side of the door, waiting for me. "No ghosts that I can see," he informed me just as a woman stepped out of an open door about halfway down the hallway.

"May I help you?"

Of average height, and in her late twenties or early thirties, she wore a sleek navy-blue sheath dress with a double row of gold buttons down the front and comfortable-looking navy pumps. Auburn hair fell in soft waves to skim her shoulders. She was professional and stunning at the same time. I was glad I'd taken care with my appearance before coming.

"I'm looking for Paul Everett."

"I'm his personal assistant." She approached in a manner that was neither unfriendly nor welcoming. "Do you have an appointment?"

Her tone implied she knew full well that I didn't. "No. I was hoping he could make time to see me. I was at the meeting last night, and I have some questions about the data center project." *And, I'd like to know where he was when Ned was murdered.* No need telling her that.

"Are you a reporter?"

"Tell her you represent a company that's interested in acquiring land in the area for a distribution warehouse."

I silently thanked Mason for his quick thinking as I repeated his words to Paul Everett's gatekeeper. "Since Haggerty Holdings owns most of the undeveloped land in the area, I thought this would be the best place to start our search for a suitable location. I won't lie," I was lying through my teeth, "this zoning battle is a concern."

The woman studied me like she had some kind of built-in lie detector. She didn't. I know this because she nodded, then told me to wait while she checked Mr. Everett's schedule. As soon as she turned her back on me, Mason chuckled. "Well done, Vi. You're a convincing liar. Should I be worried that you've been lying to me all these years?"

Mumbling under my breath, I said, "You know the meatloaf you like so well?"

"My mother's recipe?"

"The recipe she gave me tasted like dog food. Looked like it, too."

"But…"

"The woman hates me. She altered her recipe before she gave it to me. I tried it once when you were out of town and knew she'd tried to sabotage me, so I found a recipe online and added my own personal touch to it. That's what you've been eating."

"And you never said anything?" Was that admiration in his voice?

"No. What could I say? 'Hey, hon. Your mother is a vindictive witch and wants you to divorce me.' If I'd asked her about the recipe, she would have said I'd done something wrong. So, I fixed the problem and kept it to myself."

Everett's assistant reappeared in the doorway. I must have looked like a psycho, mumbling to myself in an empty hallway, but plastered on what I hoped was a serene smile as she beckoned me forward. "Mr. Everett is waiting for an important phone call, but he'll see you while he waits."

Mason answered my triumphant smirk with a wink and a grin that brought out his dimples. Grief stole my next breath, but then I saw the nameplate on the desk in the anteroom. *Natalie Everett.* My steps faltered, and I sucked in a sharp breath. I could almost feel Mason's breath on my ear as he said, "Keep it together, Vi. We'll talk about it later."

Natalie held Everett's office door open with her left hand, allowing me to pass through as well as observe the rock on her finger. It wasn't as large as the one Rhonda Haggerty wore, but I suspected it could still be seen from the space station on a clear night. Haggerty Holdings must pay its CEO extremely well to afford something like that.

The company, obviously, could afford luxury. Everett's office looked like a set director's idea of what a powerful CEO's office would look like—minus the Manhattan skyline and floor-to-ceiling glass windows. Sleek cabinetry, chrome details, and black leather accent chairs gave it a modern touch. Unfathomable monochromatic art adorned the walls, and a plush rug with black geometric designs sat atop a gray marble floor. It was as out of place in a century-old red brick mansion as a data center would be in the idyllic Pennsylvania countryside.

"Mr. Everett, this is…I'm sorry," Natalie wasn't sorry at all, "I forgot your name."

"That's because I didn't give my name." I approached the modern glass-topped desk and extended my hand. "Violet Hartwell. It's a pleasure to meet you, Mr. Everett."

Everett stood, the smile on his face morphing to confusion, then alarm as he put two and two together and came up with five. When he took a step back, I dropped my hand. "I don't want any trouble, Ms. Hartwell."

"Hartwell?" Natalie's voice could've cut glass. "Isn't she the one who murdered Ned?"

"I didn't murder anyone." I turned my attention to Paul. His face had lost all color, and he appeared to be shaking in his boots, or Italian loafers. Loafers, I think. "But I think *you* did."

"You need to leave right now, or I'll call the police." Natalie had balls enough for both of them, and clearly, Abby was right. Paul didn't have any.

"Please leave," Paul begged in a weak, trembling voice. Unless Paul suffered from a split personality, he wasn't capable of murder. Even self-defense seemed unlikely given his inability to confront me.

I'd seen enough. Keeping an eye on Mrs. Everett, I sort of sidestepped my way to the door, then bolted down the hallway and out into the clear light of day. The truck, thankfully, was steps away. Once I was safe on the open road, my brain struggled to process everything I'd learned. "He's a wimp, just like Abby said."

Mason sighed. "I wish she'd mentioned the pit bull Everett has guarding his door."

"Natalie's a piece of work, isn't she?" Needing a minute to calm my nerves, I turned into the city park and found a shaded parking spot near the picnic pavilion. I rolled the windows down and shut the engine off. No one would see me talking to myself there. "She did say his wife told him to marry her," I mused.

"You saw her. And him. Why would a woman who looks like her want a man like him?"

We spoke simultaneously. "Money."

CHAPTER TWENTY-THREE

"She didn't marry him for his money." Abby couldn't have been more adamant. "He didn't have any."

I swung by the campground and picked Bea up. Together, we'd driven to Abby's house for a little sit-down regarding Mr. and Mrs. Everett.

"How long has she been his administrative assistant?" I asked.

"Since Ned's father hired him to run the company. She was Mr. Haggerty's secretary before that."

"Don't you mean *administrative assistant*?" Bea rolled her eyes at the fancy title.

"Nope. Natalie was nineteen and fresh out of secretarial school in Philadelphia when he hired her to help him out. He was in poor health at the time. Couldn't hold a pen, so she wrote everything for him. Even signed her own paychecks."

"What?" Bea straightened in her seat. "How did she get away with that?"

"Oh, she signed Haggerty Senior's name, but it was in her handwriting. A friend of mine worked at the bank. She said there was a real ruckus the first time she tried to cash one of those checks. The bank manager called the police. They took her down to the police station so they could sort it out. Natalie convinced them to talk to Mr. Haggerty, and the old man confirmed that he'd allowed her to forge his signature. Even had her version of his name added to his signature card on file so she could sign everything for him."

"Did she have anything to do with hiring Paul?"

"I don't know, but I suspect she did. Paul was a junior account manager at the bank when all that happened. Not long after, he quit and went to work as the CEO of Haggerty Holdings."

Bea and I both whistled low. "Wow," I said. "That's quite a jump from a junior manager in a small-town bank to CEO of a large real estate company."

Bea asked, "So, she moved from being the old man's secretary to an admin assistant to the new CEO?"

Abby shook her head. "Not at first. She didn't move into that position until Rhonda left to marry Ned."

My head was spinning. "Wait," I called out. "Rhonda worked with Paul before she married Ned?"

Abby nearly doubled over with laughter. "I thought you knew that." We waited until she got herself under control. "Rhonda was Paul's secretary at Haggerty Holdings. Moved over there with him from the bank. That's how she met Ned. Paul held the purse strings of Ned's trust fund. The old man set it up so that Ned got paid at the end of the week if he turned in a timesheet from his job at the campground. No work. No pay. So, Ned came in every Friday to collect his check. It wasn't long before he and Rhonda were going out every Friday night and spending most of Ned's check. They married after a few months."

"So, Ned had to work for money from his trust?" I'd never heard of such.

"Ned worked because he liked to eat, and he liked women. Both of those required cash. But all of that ended when he got married."

"What do you mean?" Bea asked.

"Once Ned was married, he gained full access to his trust. No more guardianship." We all thought about that for a moment. Then Abby continued. "The old man died about a week after Ned and Rhonda tied the knot. Natalie moved into Rhonda's old office, and then she and Paul married soon after."

We'd gotten more information than we'd come for, so after sipping sweet tea with Abby and hearing stories from her years teaching English to ungrateful teenagers, Bea and I left. As soon as I cranked the engine on my truck, Bea asked, "What do you think about all that?"

No need to be more specific. My head was spinning with information overload as I knew hers had to be. "I have so many questions, I don't know what to ask first."

"I hear you."

At the campground, we went our separate ways. We both needed time to digest what we'd learned, and I needed to talk to Mason. I walked right through him to get a soda from the refrigerator, then sat my exhausted self down on the end of my bed. Mason and Bud joined me. "Rhonda has an airtight alibi." I popped the top on my soda and took a fortifying sip while I waited for Mason to tell me I was wrong. I so wanted to be wrong. There was a reason spouses were always the prime suspects—until they weren't. It would be so easy to clear my name if I could prove Ned's wife wasn't where she said she was at the time of his murder. Only she was.

"She didn't have a motive," Mason surmised. "She had access to all of Ned's money, and she didn't seem to care about his philandering."

"But, what if she did care? And what if those campers are wrong about the time they were in the office with her?"

Mason sighed. "They aren't wrong about the time, Vi. Rhonda didn't kill her husband."

I got up to pace the short walkway down the center of the Airstream. "Everyone seemed to think Camille was Ned's latest paramour, but we now know that's not the case." I stopped pacing and locked eyes with the ethereal being perched on my bed. "So, who was he sleeping with?"

"That's a good question, Vi." Mason's eyebrows knit. "A very good question."

"I think I'll go ask Rhonda."

Mason raised an eyebrow in question. "What makes you think she knows, or that she'd tell you if she did?"

"Really, Mason? I bet Rhonda could quote name, rank, and serial number for every woman Ned messed around with, and in chronological order." Overdressed for a visit to the campground office, I kicked my shoes off and untucked my shirt. "Everyone thinks the wife is clueless in these matters, but they never are. Pretending not to know might be easier than accepting the truth about their marriage, but trust me, they know. They *always* know." I chose a pair of purple yoga pants and a matching patterned t-shirt for my next interview. Mason remained quiet as I transformed from corporate sharpshooter to laid-back camper. It took a few minutes to gather enough laundry for a load, then I waved goodbye over my shoulder as I exited the camper.

Rhonda sat on a stool behind the counter of the camp headquarters. She gave me a withering look when I walked in, but I was on a mission to keep myself out of prison. Her grumpy attitude wasn't going to stop me from pursuing every angle possible to find out who had murdered her husband. "Got change for a ten?" I asked as I approached. "I'm out of quarters for the machines." Digging into the key slot in my yoga pants, I produced the ten-dollar bill I'd slipped in there to give me an excuse to talk to Rhonda. With pure malice in her eyes, she snatched it from my fingers. The cash register dinged, and the drawer popped open. She slapped a roll of quarters down on the counter so hard that its plastic sleeve split open. I immediately started gathering up the coins. A few went into my sports bra. I stuffed some into the same zippered compartment the bill had come from. The rest, I wrapped in my fist. As I made to leave, I "accidentally" dropped two coins and chased them down. When I stood back up, I smiled at the new widow. "Thanks. Oh, I forgot to ask who Ned's latest paramour was."

I didn't think her face could look more thunderous, but I was wrong. Her face turned a shade of red that clashed with her lipstick, and her eyes turned the color of a glacier. When she spoke, her voice was just as frosty. "Not that it's any of your business, but he was sleeping with Paul Everett's wife."

Whether it was her arctic voice or the words she'd spoken, I don't know. But my feet froze to the worn floorboards of the old building. My jaw flapped like a screen door in a storm. Mason's calm voice sounded in my head, though he was nowhere to be seen. "Say something, Vi. Thank her for the change, or something."

"Th-thanks for the change." I waved my clenched fist, and another quarter sailed across the floor. "You can keep that one." Feeling like an absolute fool, I practically ran from the building. Snatching the bag I'd left on the old wooden porch, I headed in the opposite direction from the laundry hut.

"Whoa. Slow down. People are looking at you like you've lost your marbles."

Mason was right. No one scurried around here, and I had been scurrying like a mouse with a cat on my tail. Slowing my pace, I tried to appear nonchalant when my insides rioted. Through clenched teeth, so I wouldn't look any crazier than I already did, I told Mason, "Natalie killed Ned." An image of the woman's face as she ordered me out of Paul's office sent a chill down my spine.

"Maybe," was his cautious response.

We'd reached my campsite by then. Bud bounded out as soon as I opened the door. I tossed the laundry bag inside, then waited impatiently for my canine companion to return from doing his duty. Bea and the others were nowhere in sight, and that was fine by me. I needed time to process everything I learned today. At my hand signal, Bud bounded up the steps, and I followed, shutting the door behind me. I poured myself a glass of wine from the bottle I'd left out on the counter and downed it in one gulp.

"Easy there, Vi."

"Don't lecture me about day drinking, Mason." I refilled my glass and, leaning heavily against the counter, sipped it. "It's not every day I come face-to-face with a murderer."

"You don't know Natalie Everett is the murderer."

"Did you see her? Did you *hear* her?" Still holding the glass, I pointed my index finger at my ghostly naysayer. "I was there, Mason. The woman is evil. You had to have felt it."

"All I'm saying is, she could be the killer, but without motive and opportunity, you have nothing to go on but your gut."

"I bet she heard the rumors about Ned sleeping with Camille. Right there is your motive. A scorned woman, and all."

Mason nodded as he contemplated my words. "Jealousy isn't a strong motive, but people have killed for less reason. What about opportunity? Do you know where she was when Ned was murdered?"

His question stopped my crazy train cold. "No," I admitted. "I have no idea."

"I'm not saying you're wrong, Vi. I've seen lots of murderers in my day, and she certainly seems capable of a vicious crime. Why don't you call Detective Donaldson and tell him what you found out? Maybe he already knows if she has an alibi. If she doesn't, he could go by and talk to her."

"I could ask her myself," I countered.

"Don't even think about it. Natalie could be dangerous. Let Donaldson handle it."

Rap Rap Rap "Violet? Are you in there?" At the sound of

Bea's voice, Bud jumped up and wagged his tail. She'd taken to carrying treats in her pocket and handed them out liberally.

"Just a sec," I called out. Shooing Bud back a few steps, I grabbed my laundry and shoved it into the bottom of the closet before opening the door. "Sorry. Had to clear a path. Come on in."

"Thought I heard you on the phone. I'm not interrupting, am I?"

"No. Not at all. I was just talking with an old friend." Mason shrugged at my bending of the truth. "Can I offer you a glass of wine? Or a soft drink?"

"Nah, but thanks. I just came to tell you that Earl arrested some people at the Renaissance Faire for selling drugs. It was one vendor that traveled from event to event, supplying drugs to local dealers under the guise of selling handmade pottery. Handmade in a factory in China."

"He was supplying dealers?"

"That's what Camille said, and she got it straight from Earl."

"I wonder if Ned knew? Maybe he confronted the supplier. They could have followed him and killed him to keep him quiet," I mused. Great, now I have another possible suspect.

Bea shook her head. "Not likely. Camille told me Earl wasn't the only agent monitoring the Faire. He had a couple of agents embedded to keep a close watch. Earl told Camille everyone involved in the drug business was present and accounted for at the time Ned was killed."

This was good news if I was right about Natalie, but not so good news if I was wrong. Besides those two, I had no other viable suspects. "You'll never guess what I found out today."

"Do tell."

CHAPTER TWENTY-FOUR

"Ned was having an affair with Paul Everett's wife."

"You're joking, right?" Bea's painted-on eyebrows nearly disappeared beneath her hairline, and her eyes grew big as cue balls.

"Nope." I shook my head. "Heard it straight from Rhonda's mouth, and the wife always knows."

"Well, I didn't see that coming. Did you?"

"You could have knocked me over with a feather when the widow spit out Natalie's name."

"Natalie is Paul's executive assistant. And she was the old man's secretary before that." Bea drained her wine and set the glass on the counter. "So, she knows everything there is to know about Haggerty Holdings, and was sleeping with her husband, who's the CEO, *and* Ned, who owns the company they both work for?"

"Yep. And she's a piece of work. Domineering. Ruthless. All the makings of a killer."

"Did the police even question her?"

"I doubt it. Unless someone spilled the tea about her affair with Ned, then what reason would they have to question her?"

"You need to call that handsome detective who's been hanging around. He could question her. See if she has an alibi."

"You're right." I found Donaldson's card in my purse and made the call. He seemed happy to hear from me until I told him about my visit with Mr. and Mrs. Everett."

"You did what?" I held the phone away from my ear to avoid damaging my eardrum.

"You heard me, and please don't shout at me again or I'll hang up." He grumbled an apology he clearly did not mean, and I filled him in on the reason for my call. "Did you question her, and if so, did she have an alibi?"

"I did question her, indirectly."

"What does that mean?"

"It means I went to Paul's office to question him, and she was there. Paul's alibi provided one for Natalie, too. Paul said they went home for a long lunch."

"Were you able to verify that they were at home when Ned was murdered?"

"The woman who lives across the street from them could teach Spying 101 for the CIA. She gave us the exact time they arrived and went inside, and the exact time they left."

"Was she sure they were inside the entire time?"

"She said she saw Natalie close the drapes in their bedroom about a minute after entering the house, which led me to believe they had lunch in bed."

For the life of me, I couldn't imagine those two doing anything in bed together other than sleeping, but how would I know? "Did you ask Ned what he had for lunch?"

"As I recall, I didn't ask him. He volunteered the information."

"So…what did he say?"

"He said they had sandwiches."

"Did the neighbor say anything else?"

"She said the Everetts came home for lunch several days a week."

It all sounded too convenient to me. Maybe I'd have a talk with the neighbor myself. See what else she could tell me about Ned and Natalie. "Well," I sighed, "I guess I'm back to square one."

"Don't let it get you down, Violet. I'm still looking at every angle. We'll find the real murderer. I promise."

After declining another dinner invitation from Ray, I ended the call and immediately called Abby Stump. She answered on the first ring. I didn't waste any time. "Do you know where Ned and Natalie Everett live?"

She rattled off a familiar-sounding address without having to look it up. "Thanks. And do you know who lives across the street from them?"

"My neighbor, Lydia Morris. That woman needs to find a hobby. Something besides sticking her nose in everyone else's business."

"That's why the address sounded familiar! Why didn't you tell me the Everetts live across the street from you?"

I could almost hear her shrug. "Didn't think it mattered."

Maybe it didn't. "Do you think Ms. Morris would talk to me?"

"She's got nothing else to do. What time are you thinking?"

I'd been to Abby's house. It was a short drive. "I can be there in ten minutes. Would that be okay, you think?"

"Stop by my place. We'll walk over together."

"Thanks, Abby. I'll see you soon."

Bea declined my invitation to ride along, citing the need to decide where she'd be going next and to book the campgrounds along the way. If I were allowed to leave here a free woman, my choice had been made months before Mason's death. I saw no reason to change our plans since we'd both been in agreement about what we wanted to see. The thought of being confined to a jail cell for the rest of my life made me want to curl into a ball and die.

"Don't give in to the fear, Vi." Mason always could read my emotions better than anyone else. "You're onto something here. See it through."

Adrift in an ocean of my own fears, I grasped at his encouraging words like they were a lifeline. "You think I'm onto something?"

"I do. I don't know what Natalie has to gain from Ned's death, other than maybe getting out of a bad relationship, but that alone gives her a motive."

"If Paul weren't so meek, I'd think he did it. He and Ned never got along. If he knew Ned was sleeping with his wife, that would be a motive. Not to mention, Ned was blocking the zoning on that parcel of land. Selling it for top dollar would certainly garner Paul a large bonus, maybe even a kickback from the buyer. The man has more motives than you can shake a stick at."

"True." Mason paced the confines of the trailer. "I wouldn't count him out, Vi. You never know what someone is capable of under the right circumstances."

I checked my face in the mirror on the back of the closet door, then clicked my tongue to get Bud's attention. "Come on, Buddy Boy. Let's go out." Tail wagging, he fell into step beside me. Mason blocked my path to the door. I could walk right through him, but—respect, maybe—kept me from doing it this time. I stopped short of him. "Okay, I won't count him out."

I was *so* counting Paul out.

After Bud did his business, I let him back inside the camper and promised him a treat if he was a good boy while I was away. He hopped up on my bed and settled in, giving me a sweet look that I couldn't resist. Leaning in, I kissed him on the top of his head and rubbed his ears. "I'll be back soon," I called out, as if he'd understand the concept of time.

Ms. Morris opened the door, wearing what my grandmother called a duster and a pair of fuzzy slippers. Either she cut her own hair, or she went to the local beauty school and let the wanna-be hairstylists practice on her. Her blue-gray locks hung in a lopsided pixie that made me want to tilt my head to one side when I looked at her. Her smile seemed genuine as she let us inside. Abby had called ahead to let her neighbor know we'd be dropping by. A China tea service and a plate of store-bought cookies sat next to a pair of binoculars on an oval coffee table in the living room. I sat on the end of the sofa where I had a view of the street out the front window. "Tea?" she inquired. Not waiting for a response, she lifted the pot and filled three cups. I stared at the house across the street until she waved a cup and saucer under my nose.

"Oh. Um. Thank you." I took the refreshment offered. "You didn't have to go to so much trouble. I just wanted to ask you a few questions about the people who live across the street."

"The Everetts," she confirmed with pursed lips. "Odd couple." I couldn't disagree with her assessment, so I just nodded. "What do you want to know?"

I took a tiny sip of tea, then set it on a side table. "You told the police that the Everetts came home for lunch the day Ned Haggerty was murdered."

She nodded and took a delicate sip from her cup. "Yes, I did."

Disappointment soured my stomach, or maybe it was the tea. In the back of my mind, I'd hoped she would have discovered by now that she'd been wrong and the Everetts wouldn't have an alibi. What more could I ask her? Mason's voice rang inside my head.

"She said they came home frequently for lunch. Ask her if

there was anything different about their time at home that day. Was it shorter than usual? Longer than usual? Were they wearing the same clothes when they left as they were when they arrived?"

I repeated, word for word, what Mason had said. Ms. Morris hummed and sipped at her tea as she thought back to the day in question. "You know, now that I think about it, there was something a little off that day."

Adrenaline zapped my spine straight. I did my best to sound merely inquisitive, rather than elated. "Oh?"

"Yes. When they came out of the house, they were squabbling. Bickering, I guess you could say. Since Mrs. Everett had closed the drapes in the bedroom when they arrived, I assumed they spent their lunch hour in bed. I'm old, but I remember what it was like to be young and in love. Unable to keep our hands off each other. It seemed odd that they'd be angry after doing that for as long as they did." She smiled and took another sip of tea. "I thought to myself that someone must be doing something wrong, if you know what I mean?"

"Yes, that does seem strange." Picking up on her turn of phrase, I asked, "How long were they home? Maybe it was too quick to be satisfying."

Mason practically smirked. "We had some quickies in our day, but I never left you unsatisfied." He wasn't wrong. He'd been an excellent lover, and I liked to think he didn't have any complaints where I was concerned, either.

"You know I didn't, Vi." I picked up my teacup and lifted it to my lips to hide my own smirk.

Ms. Morris shook her head. "Oh, no. Too quick wasn't the problem. They were in there for close to two hours."

Two hours? I stood and walked to the window, where I sipped the rapidly cooling tea and studied the Everetts' house. It looked similar to every other house on that side of the street. The lawn was neatly kept. The walkways and driveway were clear of debris, though a portion of the roof was covered with pine needles. I widened my gaze to include a row of tall trees across the back of the property. They were too thick to have been planted for privacy and extended as far as the eye could see up and down the block. "What's the deal with the trees behind their house? Is there a park back there?"

Ms. Morris chuckled. "No, that's the western edge of the

property Paul is trying to get rezoned."

Spinning on my heels, I pinned my gaze on Abby. "That's why you're working so hard to block the rezoning, isn't it? If it goes through, the data center would practically be your neighbor."

"There's no *practically* about it. The building would come as close to the property line as the law allows. Instead of trees, everyone on this street would be looking at concrete walls."

"But, then the data center would be in the Everett's backyard." I spun back to gaze at the majestic trees towering over the houses on that side of the street. "It doesn't make any sense. Why would Paul want to push that through?"

Ms. Morris filled us in. "Because the data center people promised to purchase his and Harvey Dreyer's houses for a small fortune. That's why." She set her cup down so hard I thought it might crack.

"Harvey Dreyer lives on that side of the street, too?"

Abby nodded to the house one down from the Everetts. "He bought that house a week before Calvin publicly announced the rezoning application."

Mason materialized in the front yard and slowly turned to face me. We locked eyes for a moment. Long enough for me to see we were on the same page. One or all of these people could be responsible for Ned's murder.

"So," I surmised, "if the zoning change goes through, everyone involved will profit except you and the other homeowners on this street?"

Abby nodded. "Rhonda will make a fortune on the sale of the land. Harvey and Paul will clean up on the sale of those houses. I suspect Calvin is looking at a huge kickback from the developer for making it all happen, but the little twerp is good at hiding his tracks."

Tracks. Trails. I gazed out the picture window at the woods beyond the row of houses. "Does anyone have a map of the hiking trails around here?"

CHAPTER TWENTY-FIVE

"Do you see what I see?"

Bea leaned over the old map I'd borrowed from Abby Stump. She traced a squiggly line with the point of her index finger. "This here's Heartbreak Trail." I held my breath as she followed the trail marked in red to where it ended on the other side of the Renaissance Faire grounds. "That's the trail you were on when you found Ned. Right?"

"Yep." I leaned in and pointed to the spot where I'd slipped off the edge of the trail and was saved from a nasty slide into the canyon by Ned's boots. Moving my finger along the line to a point midway on the trail, I pointed to a short offshoot. "And this trailhead is at the end of the cul-de-sac, three houses down from Paul Everett's house."

Bea reared back so fast you would have thought she'd been snakebit. "Seriously?"

"Seriously. And the neighborhood busybody puts Paul and his she-wolf wife at home during the time Ned was murdered. Presumably, they were doing the horizontal Mombo, but my guess is, one or both of them were out hiking." Containing my smile proved impossible. If I was right, Natalie Everett had murdered Ned Haggerty. "Natalie had motive, means, and opportunity."

"And if Paul grew a pair and turned her in, he'd lose out on the windfall coming his way."

"Exactly."

"You need to call that detective and tell him what you know."

"Not until I have proof."

"Where are you going to get that?"

"First, I'm going to take a hike. Want to come?"

She flung her arms wide, showcasing her well-worn loungewear and flip-flops. "Do I look like the hiking type?"

I chuckled. "No. I guess you don't. No worries. I just want to see how long it takes to hike from the Everetts' house to the spot where I found Ned. If I double that, I can guesstimate the round trip, plus time to confront Ned."

"Take Sherri with you. She looks like she could hold her own in a tussle."

"She's hiking on the other side of town today." I folded the map and stuck it in the only backpack I had. Elle had given it to me for my last birthday, saying the small backpacks were what everyone was carrying now instead of purses. I'd never had any use for it until now. It was just big enough to hold the map, a scaled-down version of my wallet, and my keys. I filled a water bottle from the gallon jug I kept for that purpose, and slipped my phone into the pocket designed to hold it along my right hip. Yoga pants were a marvel of technology, in my opinion. "Why don't you ride along anyway? You can drive my truck back and meet me at the trailhead here in the campground."

"I guess I could do that. That fancy truck of yours is growing on me. I might have to trade in my old Chevy one of these days."

Bea changed her shoes and grabbed the giant tote she used as a purse, and we were on our way.

After making only one wrong turn, I found the right street and the trailhead parking area. Bea leaned forward to get a look at the sky. "It's getting late. You sure you want to do this today?"

"Grab the flashlight out of the glove compartment." Mason knew better than to try to talk me out of something once I'd decided on a course of action.

Paul and Natalie should still be at the office, so it was as good a time as any to check out the hike. "I'll take a flashlight with me, just in case. There's one in the glove box." Bea located the heavy-duty light and handed it over. It wouldn't fit in my backpack with my water bottle, so I elected to carry it.

"All set," I declared as I popped the driver's side door and slid to the ground. "I'll see you back at the campground in about an hour?" I wasn't a good judge of time when it came to hiking an unknown trail. Waiting until Bea was out of sight, I backtracked along the makeshift path behind the houses until I reached the fence behind the Everetts' house. It was hard to tell if anyone had recently used the back gate in the wooden fence. The hinges showed signs of rust but not necessarily neglect. The latch was on the inside with a string to pull from the outside. I couldn't see a lock through the small crack between the gate and the fence. After a short debate with myself, which my curious side won, I tugged on the string. The latch released, and the gate jolted open a few inches before it swung shut again with a clank loud enough to set the neighbors' dogs to barking. The last thing I needed was to be arrested for snooping around, so I hightailed it out of there. Back at the trailhead, I activated the stopwatch app on my phone, waited until one minute passed to account for the time it would take Natalie to exit the yard and make it to the trailhead, then struck out at a comfortable pace.

The trail rose slowly toward the summit and the overlook where I'd literally stumbled upon the corpse. From the map Abby had loaned me, the overlook appeared to be near the midpoint along the trail. The new hiking shoes I'd purchased in town proved to be a good decision, as the narrow dirt path wound along the edge of a steep canyon, then deep into the woods before taking a sudden dip downhill. Since the trail was on private property, it was up to the landowner to maintain it. Fallen trees and crumbling edges suggested either that Ned didn't want to spend any money on the upkeep or that he left nature to its own devices to discourage hikers. Either could have been true, though from what I'd learned about the man, I suspected the latter. Someone once told me that walking downhill was more difficult than walking uphill. They were right. By the time the trail resumed its upward climb to the summit, my thighs and calves were screaming, and my toes were numb from taking the brunt of my weight against the front of the boot. A little break would do me good. I spotted an exposed boulder just off the path, and after disengaging the stopwatch, I made my way over and sat. Mason materialized beside me as I downed a refreshing drink of water from the bottle in my backpack.

"This place is beautiful. I can see why Ned and the others don't want to see it developed."

"It is beautiful," I concurred. "I think Ned died trying to protect it."

"I think you're right."

I finished off the water and returned the bottle to my backpack. I hadn't noticed the darkening sky as I'd been too busy trying to get down the steep trail without sliding down on my butt, but looking up, beyond the tree line, my impromptu stop didn't seem like such a good idea. "It's getting dark. I've got to get a move on." I didn't want to use the flashlight unless I really needed it, but it felt good to have it in my hand anyway. Just in case. In case of what, I didn't know, but lots of wildlife came out at dusk, didn't they? I'd heard there were bears, coyotes, and bobcats in the area. And God only knew what else.

"Don't worry, Vi. You've got bigger things to worry about than the local wildlife."

My heart revved like a drag racer at the starting line. "Huh?"

"Kurt is waiting for you back at the campground."

I jerked my head around to get a look at my ghostly companion. My foot slipped out from under me, and I went down hard on my hands. I lost my grip on the flashlight, and it rolled down the hill, bounced off a rock, and came to rest against the base of a large tulip poplar tree. "Argh!" Flipping over to sit on my butt, I fished my phone from my pocket and disengaged the stopwatch app again. At this rate, Bea would send out a search party for me before I even reached the summit.

"If Kurt's come to take me home like I'm a runaway child, he's gonna leave disappointed." Rather than try to stand, I inched my way down the slope until I could reach my flashlight. Thanks to a bank of clouds, the sky had darkened considerably since my last stop. I needed to pick up my pace.

"We need to get back and see what he wants."

"I'm moving as fast as I can." After dusting off my britches, I examined the flashlight. The glass lens had cracked when it hit the rock, but otherwise it appeared to be okay. Nothing happened when I pushed the power button. "Crap!" I shook it a couple of times and tried the button again. This time, it came on, and I breathed a sigh of relief. "That was a close call."

"Let's go, Vi. You need to find out why Kurt is here."

In the process of adjusting my backpack to a more comfortable position, a beam from the flashlight glinted off something about a foot behind the tree that had saved my flashlight from tumbling further down the mountain. "What's that?"

"Probably a soda can." Mason sounded perturbed. "People have no consideration for nature."

He was right. Some people had no respect for the land. Thankfully, I'm not one of them. "Might as well pack it out." Creeping closer, I squatted and swept the approximate area where I thought the object was located. Another glint had me zeroing in on the source. A low-lying branch laden with green leaves concealed the item. Pushing the limb aside, I froze when the object came into view. "Whoa!"

My skin had gone cold, but Mason's presence over my shoulder was even colder. "Don't touch it."

I rolled my eyes at the absurd order. I was already accused of stabbing Ned to death. No way was I going to pick up the murder weapon.

"That blood is fresh, Vi."

CHAPTER TWENTY-SIX

My stomach took a dive, and I fell back on my butt. Digging my heels into the dirt path, I scrambled as far away from the bloody knife as I could get. "Oh, God. Oh, God. Oh, God!" I couldn't leave the knife here, and I couldn't call the police either. If I did, they'd think I'd had an attack of conscience and provided them with the piece of the puzzle they were missing. The murder weapon. Never mind that I'd never been on this portion of the trail before today, and the fact that my fingerprints wouldn't be on the knife. They'd accused me without any evidence at all. Giving them some wouldn't help my case one iota.

"Did you hear me, Vi? The blood on that knife is fresh."

Mason's voice penetrated my spinning brain. I glanced up at him, hoping and praying he'd tell me how to get myself out of this nightmare. But instead of Mason's voice, another sent the cold chill of fear racing down my spine.

"Well, looky who we have here." Natalie Everett emerged from behind a large boulder. She was dressed like she'd stepped off the pages of an REI catalog. Her shorts alone cost more than my entire outfit, hiking boots included. Sitting on my rear, I was at a severe disadvantage, especially when she pulled a handgun from her Patagonia backpack and pointed it at me.

Paul peeked from behind her. His eyes grew wide when he saw me. "What's she doing here?"

"Who cares? She's the answer to our problem."

"Vi! Press the side button on your phone five times. Do it! Now!" It took my stunned brain a second to comprehend what

Mason was telling me. He'd drilled me and the kids on emergency tactics over and over again. My phone was still in my hand from earlier when I'd disengaged the stopwatch. Trying to be discreet, I slid my thumb along the edge until I connected with the power button. I pressed it five times, counting in my head. Help would be on the way soon. I just had to keep these two talking until they arrived.

I dug my heels in and scooted backward until my shoulder blades came up against the trunk of a tree. Using it for leverage, I got to my feet. "Hey, Natalie. Hey, Paul. I was just out for a stroll." Glancing at my wrist, I pretended surprise. "Wow! Look at the time. I'd better get going or Bea is going to call out the SRT folks."

Paul's brows knit. "SRT?"

If there was a weak link here, it had to be Paul. If I put the fear of God in him, maybe he'd convince Natalie to let me go. "Search and Rescue Team," I supplied. "Probably the police, too."

Natalie's smile reminded me of a picture I'd seen once on a nature show of a hyena laughing. Lots of teeth, but there was nothing funny about it. "That's perfect," she declared. "As a matter of fact, why don't you call them yourself?"

"What? Now?"

"Now would be good." Natalie waved the gun in the air to remind me who had the upper hand. Like I needed to be reminded.

"And tell them what? That I found the weapon used to murder Ned Haggerty, but I'm also being held at gunpoint by the woman who stabbed him?"

"You're going to tell them you've found another body at the lookout. Then you're going to hike up to the overlook and wait for them. With the bloody knife in your hand."

"What?" She wasn't making any sense. "What body?"

Natalie cut a glance at her husband, then fixed her steely gaze on me again. "Isn't that sad, Paul? She's a crazed serial killer. Talks to herself, and everything."

Talks to herself? My eyes met Mason's over Paul's shoulder. They'd overheard me talking to a ghost. There was no way to explain that away.

"Lots of people talk to themselves, Vi. It doesn't mean you're crazy."

I'm not crazy. I'm also not a serial killer. But someone here certainly was. "Who did you kill now, Natalie?"

Her laugh was maniacal. "Oh, honey, I didn't kill anyone. Paul did. But you're going to take the blame."

Paul? Was this Natalie's plan? Frame me, and if that didn't work, pin the murder, make that *murders*, on her husband? The man Calvin Dreyer bullied all through school?

"Push him, Vi. He's the weak link."

"Paul? Are you going to stand by and let Natalie throw you under the bus? Because you know that's what's going to happen, don't you? No one is going to believe I murdered *two* people I hardly knew."

If Paul shook any harder, the USGA would declare an earthquake in the region. I almost felt sorry for him until he cried out, "She made me do it!" He collapsed to his knees on the dirt path. Tears streamed down his guilt-ravaged face.

Oh. My. God. Paul *murdered Ned?*

"Shut up, you idiot!" Disgust clear in her voice, Natalie waved the gun at her husband. "You never did have any balls. I should just shoot you now and put both of us out of our misery." She aimed at her trembling target.

I'd crossed into some kind of alternate universe where nothing made sense. Paul murdered Ned *because his wife told him to*? That couldn't be right. "Who made you, Paul?"

"She did!" He pointed at his wife. "She, she said he…"

"He what?" I prodded.

"Shut. Up!" Natalie took a step closer to Paul. At that distance, she couldn't miss if she pulled the trigger.

"He said the baby wasn't his!"

"What baby?"

"You idiot! Shut. Up!" Natalie waved the gun in Paul's face. Her hand trembled with rage. "We can still make this work if you'll just shut up!"

"Make what work?" Where were the cops? The last rays of sunlight glinted off the blade of the knife in the bushes, a grim reminder that these two were possibly responsible for yet another murder. Natalie teetered on the edge of sanity.

"Pick up the knife!"

Holding both hands up, I backpedaled. "Okay. Okay. I'll get the knife."

Mason's voice in my head gave me hope. "Donaldson is almost here. Do what she says, but move slowly."

Lowering my rear end to the steep path, I crept toward where they'd hidden the knife.

"Hurry up, you purple cow! We haven't got all night!"

Purple cow? I glared at the woman. "That was uncalled for."

"Vi! What are you doing?"

"You've been nothing but trouble since the day you pulled that aluminum Twinkie of yours into the campground. Nobody was supposed to find Ned for days. Weeks maybe. By then, the zoning change would be a done deal, and a simple DNA test would prove my baby was his. Paul would push the land sale through, and this kid would inherit enough money to keep me in style for the rest of my life." With the gun pointed my way, Natalie advanced toward me. "But, no." She dragged out the last syllable. "You had to stumble on his body that very afternoon. Thanks to you, I'll be stuck with Paul for the rest of my life."

"You were going to pin the murder on him, weren't you?"

She sneered, showing off her unnaturally white teeth. "Of course I was! He murdered the man who got his wife pregnant! It was the perfect setup. Until you came along."

"I didn't know she was pregnant! I swear I didn't! She *made me* stab Ned. She said he was going to fire me if the zoning went through. He had to be stopped!"

Natalie swung the barrel of the gun back toward her husband. "How many times do I have to tell you to shut up?"

Paul rambled on. "Ned had all that money, and he didn't even want it! It wasn't fair!"

"You idiot! We can still have it all if you'll just stop talking."

"What about Rhonda and Camille? Ned's wife and daughter?" She pointed the gun at me again. I was within reach of the knife now, but instead, I closed my hand around my flashlight that rested in the same place as before. Thankfully, my purple cow body blocked the movement from Natalie's view. Score one for women who eat brownies for breakfast.

"Accidents happen. Rhonda should take better care of her car. And Ned's so-called daughter? Corpses can't inherit."

My blood ran cold. "What have you done?"

"I didn't want to kill her!" Paul's tearful confession drew his wife's attention his way again. "She made me! She said she'd kill me if I didn't stab that woman!"

Picturing Camille's young, smiling face in my mind, my

stomach revolted at the idea of her lying out here somewhere, bleeding to death. These two had murdered her. For what? She didn't need Ned's money and wouldn't have kept it if any had come her way. I gripped the flashlight so hard my hand cramped. They had to be stopped.

"Vi? Donaldson is here. He's a few feet behind Paul, in the woods." Thank the Lord. It was time to end this and, hopefully, save Camille's life.

Nodding that I'd heard Mason, I cried out. "You murdered Camille?" As predicted, Natalie turned the gun on me. The instant she did, I raised the flashlight and pushed the power button. I dropped my shoulder to the trail and rolled, just as she pulled the trigger.

CHAPTER TWENTY-SEVEN

What happened next is a blur. A shadowy figure darted out of the woods and tackled Natalie to the ground. Her shot missed me but splintered a nearby sapling. Whether she intended to fire again or did so reflexively upon being taken down, her second shot had better luck finding a target. It connected with Paul's shoulder. Already on his knees, he fell face-first into the dirt where his tears mixed with blood from the wound.

On her stomach, wrists cuffed behind her back, Natalie went all in on her plan to throw her husband under the speeding bus. "He did it! It was him! Paul killed them both!"

Suddenly, the small patch of trail swarmed with uniformed police officers. Flashlight beams swept the area. Several landed on me as I attempted to right myself. A kid no older than my twins offered me a hand and helped me to my feet. "Detective Donaldson? She's over here."

Donaldson relinquished Natalie to another officer, and after making sure the EMTs were on their way for Paul, he came to check on me. Or maybe he came to arrest me. Who knew? "What happened here, Violet?" Was that amusement I heard in his voice?

"Uh…well, I was out for a hike."

He held a hand up like a stop sign. "Whoa. Hold it right there. Bea called me. I know exactly why you were out here. What I don't know is how you got mixed up with those two." He motioned to the husband-and-wife murder team. "And what did Mrs. Everett mean when she said her husband murdered them both?"

"Oh, no! Quick! You have to go check on Camille! Natalie

said she was at the lookout. They stabbed her and hid the knife over there." I pointed to the tree that had twice stopped my flashlight from rolling down the mountain. "Please hurry! She might still be clinging to life!"

Donaldson directed an officer to shine his light where I'd indicated. He bent down, then abruptly stood. He instructed the officer. "Bag that as evidence." Turning, he pointed at two other officers. "You two, double-time it up to the overlook. There might be a stabbing victim up there. Her name's Camille Stone. Her husband reported her missing an hour ago. Keep your eyes peeled on the way in case she stumbled this way looking for help."

The paramedics arrived and were tending to Paul when Donaldson's radio crackled to life. "We've got her, Detective. She's alive but needs medical attention ASAP."

"Stay with her. Help is on the way." After verifying that Paul's gunshot wound wasn't life-threatening, Donaldson sent the medical team up the trail to see what they could do for Camille.

Once he'd sent Natalie and Paul down the way I'd come, he circled back to me. It didn't escape my notice that we were alone in the woods. Without a dozen or so flashlights illuminating the darkness, my night vision had improved enough that I could see the expression on the detective's face. Mason used to look at me that way when I did something crazy that somehow turned out all right. Like the time I painted the pergola in our backyard purple. He'd been totally against it, but I'd taken on the project as a way to distract myself from worrying about him while he was away on a case. After being gone for two weeks, he'd come home late at night and gone straight to bed. The next morning, I found him with a cup of coffee in his hands, staring out the kitchen window at the newly painted structure. There was no need to say anything. It was impossible to miss. I got myself a cup of coffee and joined him. At long last, he faced me, and there was that look. Part amusement. Part concern. Part annoyance. I kept my mouth shut and let him work through his thoughts on the subject. Finally, he tipped my chin up, gazed into my eyes, and uttered the only words he'd ever say on the subject. "I'm sorry you worried about me, Vi." Then he kissed me, and all was right between us again.

One thing I knew for certain—Detective Donaldson wasn't going to kiss me. I wasn't ready for a relationship. Not with Mason looking over the man's shoulder. "Is Camille going to be okay?" I asked.

"The officers aren't doctors, but they seemed to think they found her in time. I hope they're right."

"I hope so, too. She didn't deserve this."

"No one deserves to be stabbed and left for dead, Violet." Placing his hands on his hips, he glared at me. "Why didn't you call me and tell me what you suspected? I would have come out here with you."

He wasn't going to like my answer, but there was no way to sugarcoat the truth. "I didn't think you'd take me seriously. Besides, all I was going to do was clock how long it would take Natalie to hike from her house to the overlook. How was I to know she and Paul were out on another killing spree?"

Donaldson huffed out a frustrated breath. "You couldn't have known that, but murderous couples aside, you had to know it was going to get dark before you got to the campground. You shouldn't have been out here alone."

"I brought a flashlight." I waved its bright beam around to prove my point. "And I would have been back at the campground a long time ago if I hadn't…" Uh oh. Admitting this whole thing started because I slipped and lost my flashlight would prove Donaldson's point. Unfortunately for me, the detective seized on my slip.

"If you hadn't, what, Violet?"

"Tell him, Violet." I made a face at Mason. Donaldson picked up on that as well.

"What was that face for?"

Darn it. I'd hoped he hadn't seen that. The man had eyes like a hawk. Or maybe an owl. A skyward glance revealed the moon and stars obscured by low-lying clouds, which explained the depth of darkness surrounding us. A couple of flashlight beams appeared on the trail below us, coming our way. "Looks like the CSI folks are here. We'd better get out of their way." Retrieving my mini-backpack from the ground beside my left foot, I tried to step around the broad-shouldered detective.

"Oh, no, you don't." He grabbed me by the arm, halting my forward progress. "What happened out here, Violet?"

Sighing, I let the backpack dangle from my fingertips. I guess he took my relaxed stance as confirmation that I wasn't going to dart off and let go of my arm. "It was nothing, Detective. I slipped on the steep upgrade and dropped my flashlight. It rolled down the trail and came to a stop next to that tree." I pointed to the spot in question. "I scooted on my bum until I could reach it, and that's when I saw the knife. Natalie and Paul came out of hiding then, and well, you know the rest."

"Did you touch the knife?"

"Do I look like an idiot? No. I didn't touch the murder weapon. I did, however, record their confessions."

"How did you do that?"

"The same way I called for help. With my phone." I retrieved the device from the side pocket of my yoga pants and handed it over. "I'd like that back as soon as possible, please."

This time, he didn't stop me from leaving. The crime scene techs scowled at me when I passed them by, but I didn't stop to chat with them. Donaldson could explain my presence—or not. I was done.

A circus of red and blue strobe lights greeted me at the trailhead. Only then did I realize I should have gone the other way on the trail. Bea had my truck at the campground end, and I had no way to call her, having handed my phone over to the annoying detective.

Speak of the devil. "Come on, Violet. I'll give you a ride back to the campground."

"Give me my phone and I'll call Bea to come get me."

"Your phone is evidence now."

"I won't erase the conversation I recorded. Promise." I made a show of crossing my heart.

"No can do, Hartwell." Donaldson started walking, and I followed.

CHAPTER TWENTY-EIGHT

"That wasn't so hard, now was it?" he asked as we pulled out of the cul-de-sac.

"I'm not talking to you without my lawyer present." Which was ridiculous since I'd told him everything I knew back on the trail.

"In light of this new evidence, I feel confident in saying the charges against you will be dropped soon."

"Not soon enough."

"Where will you go next?"

Mason had made reservations for us at a campground near Philadelphia, but after my experience here, I was in the mood for a quieter place. I answered truthfully. "I don't know. Just away from here."

There wasn't much he could say to that, so he didn't. Silence filled the car until we arrived at my campsite. A vehicle with D.C. plates blocked my pickup in. Bea stood between a man and the door to my camper. Bud sat beside her, his teeth bared. "Oh. My. Lord." I reached for the door handle. I'd forgotten all about Kurt being here.

"Isn't that your lawyer?" Donaldson joined me at the hood of his car.

"No. I fired him right after the arraignment."

"What's he doing here then?"

"Good question." I weaved my way past Kurt's Beemer and around the back of my truck. When I was close enough to be heard over Bud's growling, I called out. "What are you doing here?" At the sound of my voice, Mason's best friend turned to face me. Before he'd come to my rescue, then insulted me and my late husband for our decision to see the country one campground at a time, I would have fallen for his easy smile and confident swagger. But not now. There was something off about the way the man tried to manipulate me into returning to my old life when he knew full well I was living my and Mason's dream.

Hands held out in supplication, he pleaded his case. "Can't a friend check up on another friend?"

"I don't trust him, Vi. He could have called to check on you. There was no need to drive all this way."

Hearing Mason voice my thoughts gave me courage. I approached with caution. Bud ran to my side, brushing up against my leg. "You could have called, Kurt. My phone number hasn't changed."

If men had hackles, the second Kurt spotted Detective Donaldson, his went up. It was like one of those toys M.J. used to love. The FBI agent transformed from a doting, concerned friend to a junkyard dog in the blink of an eye. Bud resumed growling at him. Or maybe that was Kurt growling. Hard to tell. "If you were going to replace Mason, Vi, you should have told me. I guarantee you'd have a better time in my bed that his." If looks could kill, Donaldson would be dead. And if ghosts could touch the earthly realm, Kurt would be out cold on the ground. In all our years together, I'd never seen Mason strike out in anger at anyone. Until now.

"I'm going to kill him. I swear, Vi, I'm going to rise from the grave and kill him if he so much as lays a hand on you."

"What is wrong with you, Kurt? I have no intention of replacing Mason with anyone, least of all you." I shook my head, hoping the motion would shake all the disjointed pieces of this mess into some sort of meaningful order. "Mason would be appalled to hear you speak to me that way. You were supposed to be his best friend."

Donaldson closed the distance between us and stood by my side. "I'm sure a big shot FBI agent like you wouldn't remember, but we met before. I'm Detective Ray Donaldson with the local PD. I was just returning Ms. Hartwell home after she was nearly murdered up on the mountain. So, unless you have something constructive to say to her, I think you need to be on your way.

Violet has been through enough already tonight."

"I like this guy, Vi."

Shut up, Mason.

"What do you mean, almost murdered?" Bea screeched.

"It's a long story," I said to ease her worries. "I'll tell you later."

Kurt sneered at Donaldson. "I remember. You're the nitwit who arrested Violet for a crime she didn't commit. If anyone needs to leave, it's you."

"Kurt. Stop." This was getting out of hand. "Detective Donaldson was under orders from his chief. He never thought I was guilty. He caught the real perpetrators tonight. So, if you're here to offer your legal services again, I don't need you."

Bea spoke up. "I already told him that, but he was adamant he was going to wait inside your trailer for you."

"My door is locked, Kurt. How did you plan to get in?"

"I'd like to hear this, too," Donaldson chimed in.

"Oh, come on, Violet," Kurt scoffed. "Anyone with a can opener could get into that tin can. I still can't believe Mason would want you living in that thing all alone."

"I'm not alone. I have Bud, and I'm surrounded by friends." I scratched the dog behind his ear and smiled at Bea, who crossed her arms over her ample bosom and nodded enthusiastically.

"They're formidable opponents. I'll give you that, but they're no match for a person with a gun." As if he realized he wasn't getting anywhere with his current line of B.S., he transformed once again. His shoulders slumped, and his expression softened. "Elle called me, Vi. She's worried about you. She and M.J. think you should come home. I'll give you tonight to think about it, and I'll be back in the morning to help you hook up the trailer. I'll drive your truck home, and you can drive my car."

"How many times do I have to say it, Kurt? I'm not going back to my old life. Mason is gone, and there's nothing to go back to. Elle and M.J. understand. As a matter of fact, when I spoke to them both *yesterday*, they suggested I sell the house. Neither one said anything about wanting me to return home."

"He's lying, Vi. I don't know why, but he is."

Mason wasn't saying anything I didn't already know. Beyond exhaustion, all I wanted to do was crash for the night. Tomorrow would be soon enough to plan my next steps and savor my newly acquired freedom. "Please leave, Kurt. I've made up my mind. I'm going to complete the trip Mason and I planned. After that, I'll decide if I'm going back or not."

He took a step closer, his hands outstretched again to plead his case. Bud stood and growled at him. "If you insist on completing the trip, then for God's sake, stay in hotels. I'll take the trailer home, and you can have my car for as long as you need it."

"I don't know how many times I have to say it, Kurt. No. No. No."

Donaldson got in the man's face. "The lady has made herself clear, Mr. Landis, so it's time for you to move along."

"That's Agent Landis to you." Kurt stomped toward his car and climbed behind the wheel. Before backing out, he rolled down the window and called out, "You're making a mistake, Violet. You'll see. It won't be long before you'll be begging me to help you again."

Bea stood beside me and the detective as we watched Kurt's taillights disappear into the night. "What's with that guy? And why does he want to get his hands on your trailer?"

"Huh?" I stared at the older woman. "What do you mean?"

"I don't think he's worried about you in the least. Before you got here, he insisted it would be better if he waited for you inside. Who does that?" She shook her head. "The man is determined to get his hands on your trailer. Makes no sense." Glancing between me and Donaldson, Bea raised one eyebrow and smirked. "I can see I'm not needed here. I'll be over in the morning with coffee, and you can tell me everything that happened tonight. And by everything, I mean *every. Thing.* Goodnight, everyone." She waved over her shoulder as she made her way to the adjacent campsite. Donaldson and I watched until she was safely inside her camper.

"Well, I guess I'll be going." Donaldson dug his keys out of his pocket. "You sure you're going to be okay?"

I gave him a tired smile. "I'm sure. And thanks for the ride home, and for sticking around to make sure I was alright."

"It's part of the job." He tossed his keys in the air and then caught them. "I'll make sure the charges against you are dropped tomorrow. Call if you need anything."

CHAPTER TWENTY-NINE

"Bea's right, Vi." Mason stared at our Airstream. "Kurt's interest in the trailer isn't normal."

"Granted, he's being an ass, but what could he possibly want with our camper? His definition of roughing it is staying in a 4-star hotel." I signaled Bud to go do his business while I unlocked the trailer. I left the door open for the dog as I turned on the light above the sink and then kicked my shoes off. Bud bounded in, and I closed and locked the door.

"Maybe it would be better if you deviated from our planned route."

"You gave Kurt a copy of our itinerary?"

"Seemed like the right thing to do at the time. We were working on several open cases. I didn't want to be completely out of touch."

I shed my dirty clothes, pulled on my favorite pajamas, and then stepped into the tiny bathroom to brush my teeth. I squeezed a dab of paste on my toothbrush, then peeked in the mirror, expecting to see Mason's reflection over my shoulder. Seeing only the open shower behind me, I glanced into the hallway at my husband's ghost. "So now you think *I* should be completely out of touch?"

Mason shrugged. "Wouldn't hurt to change things up a bit. You can let the kids know so they won't worry."

Leaning over the tiny sink, I brushed my teeth and then rinsed. A chill brushed across my skin as I stepped through the apparition to turn off the lights in the front and double-check that I'd locked the door. When I approached, Bud scooted to the foot of the bed, and I crawled under the covers. Mason settled beside me. "I guess it's a good thing I already decided I'm not going to the Philly campground then."

"When did you decide this?"

"On the way home tonight. After all that happened here, I could use some peace and quiet."

"What do you have in mind?"

"Don't know yet. I have some ideas, though." I pulled the covers up around my neck and willed my wired body to relax. "I'm going to take a few days to think about it."

"You do that, Vi. You do that."

Bud nuzzling my face alerted me to someone knocking on my door. According to the light streaming around the edges of my blackout blinds, a new day had dawned some time ago. Swinging my feet to the floor, I yawned and stretched before calling out, "Hold your horses! I'll be right there."

A quick peek through the window over the sink brought a groan to my lips. Making new friends was both a blessing and a curse. The women gathered outside had believed in my innocence and stood by me through the entire ordeal. I owed them a lot, but I was not ready to face them this morning. Weeks of stress on top of my ever-present grief had taken a toll on me.

Bud bounded past me, his tail wagging as he expected to be let out. There was no way I could hold him prisoner just so I could hide out, so I flicked the latch and pushed the door open. Bud barreled down the steps and into the throng of women waiting for me to make an appearance. I stood in the open portal, unapologetic about my appearance. Unlike the women I had called friends in my old life, these didn't care if my hair was sleep-frazzled, or if I had a pillow crease on my cheek, or if my pajamas were serviceable cotton instead of silk. I was going to miss them when I moved on. "Hey there. Give me a minute and I'll be right out."

By the time I dressed, fed Bud, and made myself a cup of coffee, a minute had turned into twenty. The gang had brought their own lawn chairs and gathered beneath my canopy, waiting for me.

Mille held out a pink box. "Have a donut. I picked up enough for everybody at the bakery in town." I helped myself to a chocolate-covered one. "You're the talk of the town, Vi."

I almost choked on the bite I'd taken of the confectionery goodness. "I am?"

"The story made the paper." Bea held up a copy of the local paper. The front-page headline read, "Local Couple Arrested for Murder!" Taking the paper from her, I scanned the lengthy article that quoted Detective Donaldson as saying the police were certain they now had the individuals responsible for the murder of Ned Haggerty and the attempted murder of his daughter, Camille Stone.

"How's Camille? Has anyone heard?"

Kendra wiped powdered sugar from her lips with the back of her hand. "I talked to Earl this morning. He came by their trailer to pack some things for her. He said she's out of surgery and is expected to make a full recovery. Paul's initial thrust caused her to lose her footing, and she fell over the edge of the overlook before he could stab her again. Unlike you, Ned's body wasn't there to stop her, so she tumbled quite a way down the slope, and her assailants left her for dead. The knife wound bled a lot, but, thankfully, didn't cause any major damage. She has a broken arm from the tumble and a bunch of scratches and bruises. Earl said to tell you thanks. If you hadn't been out there on your fact-finding mission, no one would have had any idea what had happened to Camille. She probably would have died before someone found her."

"You're a hero," Millie said with a smile in her voice.

"No." I shook my head. "I was just in the right or the wrong place at the right time. I'll have to go see Camille before I leave here." Something regarding Camille's search for her birth parents had been nagging at me ever since she mentioned the situation to me. I could be entirely off base, but I wouldn't know that until I asked a few more questions.

Sherry offered me another donut, but I was still working on my first one and declined. "What are you going to do now that you're free of the murder rap?"

"Have any of you heard of a website that matches campers up with vineyards during harvest time? The farmers offer free camping in return for help harvesting the grapes."

Willa practically bounced out of her seat. "I have! I signed up to help at a vineyard in New Jersey next month. You should come. I'm sure they have room for more campers."

"I did it once," Sherry offered. "At a vineyard in Virginia. It was hard work, but only for a few days. Not only did they let me camp for free on their land, but they paid me in wine. It was good wine, too." She noticed I'd finished my donut and offered the box again. I took an apple fritter this time.

"I've never done anything like that," I admitted, "but how difficult can it be? You just snip the grape clusters off the vines, right?"

"Yep," Sherry confirmed. "It can be backbreaking, depending on which variety of grapes you're harvesting. Sometimes you have to lean over to find the clusters, but yeah, it's a pretty mindless activity."

After what I'd been through, a mindless activity sounded pretty darn good. I pointed at Millie. "Can you send me a link to the website you used, and the name of the vineyard you're going to? I think I'll join you if they have room for one more."

"Absolutely!" She pulled her phone from her back pocket. "I'm so excited! This is going to be a blast!"

I didn't share her enthusiasm, but I was proud of myself for making a decision on my own. I could return to our original itinerary, but the next adventure would be of my own choosing. The change in direction would also keep Kurt off my trail. My phone chimed with a text I assumed was from Millie until I retrieved it from where I'd left it on the counter just inside the camper door. "It's from my lawyer. She said we have a court date tomorrow afternoon to formally drop the charges against me, but to consider myself free of them as of now."

A chorus of cheers rose from my new friends as I collapsed into my camp chair. Even though I'd been expecting the charges to be dropped, tears welled in my eyes at the news.

"This calls for a celebration!" Bea stood. "Party at my place. Tonight. Everybody is invited!"

We were all on our feet, everyone talking at once, offering to bring something or do something for the party. "You," Bea pointed at me. "Just bring yourself and Bud. We've got the rest."

Unable to speak, I nodded, accepting that the party was in my honor. I didn't deserve it, but a celebration *was* in order. The group dispersed, and I went inside to call Elle and M.J. They hadn't heard about last night, and I wasn't about to tell them how close I'd come to being another victim of the murderous couple. All that was behind me.

"They do worry about you, you know?"

"I know. And I worry about them, too. They're still so young, Mason."

"We were engaged and living together when we were their age," he reminded me.

"Well, the world was a different place back then. The potholes we navigated around have grown into craters filled with monsters." I shook my head. "Life was so much simpler when all I had to worry about was diaper rash and which preschool to send them to." My gaze met his. "And you. Every time you walked out the door to go to work, I worried."

His smile was tender, his gaze warm. "I never wanted you to worry about me, Vi. You know that. I did everything I could to make sure I came home to you and the twins." Mason turned his back on me, but not before I saw the shift in his countenance. "Then something like this happens, and in the blink of an eye, I did the unthinkable and left you all alone. It makes no sense, Vi. None of it makes sense."

I reached out, wishing I could touch him, comfort him, but my fingers met with cold, empty air.

CHAPTER THIRTY

The moment the judge's gavel finalized his decision, a cheer rose from the back of the courtroom. Mason shot me a thumbs-up along with a smile filled with love and pride. I smiled back even as my shoulders sagged in relief. I was officially free again, and I'd made a bunch of new friends I wanted to keep in touch with. Avery Simmons, the public defender who'd been assigned to my case after I fired Kurt, gave me a warm hug. "Easiest case, ever," she said, stepping back to gather her things. "For the record, I never thought you did it."

"That's kind of you to say, and I can't thank you enough for stepping in when you did."

Avery stuffed the last of her papers into her leather briefcase, then leaned heavily on the scarred oak defense table. "What are you going to do next?"

"I'd like to hear that myself." Detective Donaldson pushed through the swinging gate that separated the audience from the court proceedings. He wore a dark blue suit, which he probably reserved for court appearances, along with a sky-blue shirt and a striped tie. If I were interested in a relationship, I could do worse than hook up with a man like him.

"I was thinking I'd take myself and the Hitchin' the Road Ladies out to lunch to celebrate. Both of you are invited."

Avery's brows knit. "The Hitchin' the Road Ladies?"

I waved to the women in the back row. They enthusiastically waved back. "My friends from the campground. They all tow their own trailers, so you know, hittin' the road/hitchin' the road?"

"I get it." Avery smiled and waved back. "Text me where you'll be. I've got some paperwork to take care of here in the courthouse. I'll join you afterward, if that's okay?"

"Absolutely." I gave her another hug, then watched as she exited the courtroom. I turned my attention to Ray Donaldson. "You coming?"

"Nah, but maybe we could meet for coffee later?"

"I'd like that. I have some questions I'd like to ask you."

"Oh? About what?" He took my elbow and steered me away from the table as the next defendant and his attorneys moved in.

"Just questions. You've lived here a long time, right?"

"Longer than I thought I would."

I grinned at his reply. Life had a way of sneaking up on you. "You like it here. Don't even think about saying otherwise."

"Come on. We've got to get out of here."

I followed him up the aisle, signaling for my friends to follow us out the door. Once outside on the courthouse steps, I made arrangements to meet Ray for coffee mid-afternoon at a local eatery. As soon as he was gone, the Hitchin' the Road Ladies wrapped me up in a giant hug, complete with squeals and shouts of, "We did it!" I laughed and cried, and hugged them one by one, thanking them for their unwavering support.

"Ladies, let's celebrate. Lunch and drinks are on me!"

***

Still riding high from being exonerated, I returned to the campground and took Bud for a short walk before loading him up in the truck and driving back into town to meet Detective Donaldson. I'd purposely chosen a place with outdoor seating so I could bring my dog along. Nothing says *we're only here to talk* like having a canine chaperone.

"You could have left him with Bea." Mason lounged in the front passenger seat. "Then this could have been a real date."

"Give it up, Mason. I'm not interested in dating anyone."

"Then why did you agree to meet him today?"

I slowed to make the sharp turn onto Main Street. "I have a hunch about Camille's birth mother, and I think he may know something about that."

"This isn't your business, Vi."

"No, it's not, but I like Camille, and I feel sorry for her. She found and lost her birth father in a few weeks' time. I have a hunch about who her birth mother is, and I'm going to follow up on that hunch."

"You're a softie, Vi."

"I'll take that as a compliment."

"It is one. Your soft heart is what drew me to you in the first place. It's one of your best qualities."

Donaldson stood outside the restaurant as I drove by. I swung around the corner and found a pull-in parking space I could navigate with the enormous truck and parked. "Come on, Bud. Let's get this over with." Mason vanished as Bud leaped over the center console and landed in the passenger seat, his tail wagging, and tongue hanging out with excitement. The detective waved when he saw me approach.

"Detective Donaldson," I smiled in greeting. "Long time no see."

He bent to greet Bud with a head rub. "I see you brought your chaperone."

"I don't know what you're talking about, detective. Bud is my bodyguard."

"And I'm the King of England."

We entered the outdoor seating area through a break in the wrought-iron fencing. I chose a shaded seat along the outside where there was more room for Bud to lie down. A waitress appeared within moments with menus and a carafe of water for the table. We ordered coffee and two desserts to share.

Donaldson watched as I pulled out Bud's collapsible water dish, filled it from the carafe, and placed it on the concrete where he could reach it. "Where did you get him?" he asked.

"At the local Humane Society. They told me someone found him walking on the side of the road and called them."

"He's a lucky dog."

"I'm the lucky one. He's a great companion, and he likes to ride in the pickup with me."

Our desserts and drinks arrived. We dug in, avoiding conversation as long as possible. At least, that was my excuse for being mute. When the plates were cleared and our mugs refilled, I jumped in with both feet. "I have a theory about Camille Stone's birth mother."

Donaldson eyed me over the rim of his mug. "And you think I can help you with that?"

"Maybe. Did you know Ned when he was in high school?"

"No."

Darn it. "What about Beverly Carson? How well do you know her?"

He squared his shoulders, and his gaze bore into mine. "Why do you ask?"

I sipped my coffee and then carefully set the mug on the table. "Because I think she might be Camille Stone's birth mother."

"Again, I can't help you with that."

"Why not?" The slight lift of his left shoulder and the way he glanced across the street rather than meet my gaze told me what I needed to know. "You dated her, didn't you?"

"Maybe." He took another sip, then cradled the mug in both hands. "Okay. Yes. For a hot minute, and by hot, I mean short. We went out a couple of times. The movies. Dinner. A legal secretary and a cop. It should work, right?"

"I guess."

"Well, it didn't. We had zero chemistry, and since neither one of us could talk about our work, we had nothing to say to each other."

"I don't guess you ever got around to talking about your previous relationships?"

"You'd guess right."

"So, you don't know if she gave birth to Ned's baby when she was a teenager?"

"I don't know." He stared into the distance for a moment. "I guess it's possible. She let me in when I came to pick her up for our second date. She has a picture of her and Ned, all dressed up, on a shelf in her living room. I asked her about it. She said it was her prom picture, and that she kept it there because it made her laugh every time she saw it. You've seen prom pictures. Kids trying to look like adults. It was humorous."

"I bet it is." I studied my cooling coffee and let his story sink in.

"Sorry, I can't help you. I hope Camille finds her birth mother. After what she's been through, she deserves a happy ending."

I nodded. "She does, but not all birth parents want to be found. There's no guarantee whoever it is will be receptive to meeting Camille."

"I suppose you're right." Donaldson signaled for our check. "Maybe you should stay out of it. If the woman wants to be found, she probably would have contacted Camille by now. Everyone in town knows who she is and why she's here."

"You're probably right. I don't know Camille's actual birthday. It's possible her mother is someone Ned met in college. Or maybe someone passing through that he had an affair with."

The waitress brought our check. I offered to pay all or half, but Ray — yes, I was now calling him Ray—whipped a couple of bills out of his wallet and handed them over before I could retrieve my purse from where Bud was using it as a pillow.

Before we parted ways, I thought to ask, "What are the chances of getting my things back from when you searched my trailer?"

"We didn't take much."

"I know, and I don't care about any of it, other than my coffee mug. It was a gift from my kids when they were little. It has sentimental value."

"I'll see what I can do."

"Thank you. And thanks for getting the check. I appreciate it."

On the sidewalk, Ray leaned in and placed a chaste kiss on my cheek. In true Donaldson fashion, he turned and walked away without looking back.

"You haven't seen the last of him."

"Shut up, Mason."

CHAPTER THIRTY-ONE

I couldn't leave town without seeing for myself that Camille was okay, but I had another stop to make before I did. A quick search on my phone gave me the names and addresses of the only two attorneys in town. A deeper search revealed the office where Beverly Carson worked. Since it was only a short walk from the restaurant, I elected to leave my cumbersome vehicle where it was and go on foot. Bud seemed to like the idea, so using a mapping app, we took off to see a woman about a secret baby.

The sign on the door showed the office would close soon. The reception desk was empty, so I called out as I inched my way down the hall. "Beverly? It's me, Violet Hartwell."

I heard footsteps, then Beverly appeared in a doorway on the left, about midway down. Unlike the first time I'd seen her at the Renaissance Faire, this time she wore a smart, cream-colored suit with a pale blue blouse and matching pumps. Her makeup was flawless, and her jewelry understated. I imagined the prom photo Donaldson had described and thought the woman had grown in style and confidence in the intervening years. Recognizing me, she smiled. "Oh, hi. To what do I owe this pleasure?"

I glanced around and, seeing no one, asked, "May we talk in private?"

She waved me into her office and shut the door. "What's this about?"

Giving her what I hoped was an understanding look, I said, "I think you know."

Beverly slid behind her desk and, slowly, as if she might

break, lowered herself into her chair. More than ever, I thought I was right about her. "Really? I don't have a clue why you're here."

I gingerly perched on the edge of the visitor's chair facing her desk. "Camille Stone." The color drained from Beverly's face. I continued. "She's your daughter. Yours and Ned's."

She picked up a pen and clamped both hands around it so tightly it's a wonder it didn't break. "Why would you think that?"

"Besides the obvious way you still carried a torch for Ned, she has your eyes."

"She does?" Catching herself, she backtracked. "That's impossible. I don't have any children."

"I'm not judging you, Beverly. I'd never do that. Young women often find themselves in untenable circumstances and are forced to make decisions that go against everything their heart tells them. I can't even imagine the strength it took to do what was right for your daughter. Trust me when I say Camille is grateful to you. She's had a wonderful life, but like many adopted children, she's always felt like something was missing."

Perhaps realizing I hadn't come to stand in judgment, Beverly sank back in her chair, the weight of her past bearing down on her shoulders. "How did you figure it out?"

"Like I said. It was the way you spoke about Ned, and a friend mentioned he'd seen the prom photo at your house. Then, the eyes. She really does have your eyes."

For the longest, the only sound in the small office was the whir of the air conditioning as it cycled on and off. Beverly had lived with her secret for almost thirty years. Revealing it now would take as much, if not more, courage than it had taken for her to give birth alone, then give her child up. It was Beverly who broke the silence. "I watched the church for weeks. Even attended services there a few times. The women were a chatty bunch, eager to gossip about the childless couple to a young, pregnant girl. Pastor Barnes and his wife were kind, generous people, by all accounts. Marilyn even told me once how much she envied me. She and Timothy hadn't been able to conceive, you see." Not trusting my voice, I nodded. Beverly went on. "So, I watched. Stalked might be a better word. I knew what time Marilyn arrived at the church every Sunday to arrange the altar flowers. So I waited, and when Camille was three weeks old, I wrapped her up in a pretty pink blanket I'd bought at a thrift store. I pinned a note on the blanket with her name on it. Camille Rose, after my mother, Camille, and Ned's mother, Rose. Then I hid and watched to make sure Marilyn was the one who found her. If anyone else had picked her up, I would have rushed over and snatched her out of their hands. But Marilyn was right on time, and I knew the moment she saw Camille that I'd made the right decision. Her face lit up with so much love."

Tears ran unchecked down Beverly's cheeks as she revisited that momentous day. "I cried for weeks. I missed so many classes that I almost flunked out of school. I'd hidden the pregnancy well, so none of my professors questioned me when I told them I'd been sick. Most let me turn in assignments late. Others weren't so accommodating." She sighed and swiped tears with the palm of her hand. "But you didn't come here to listen to my sob story." Her gaze locked with mine. "What do you want?"

"Nothing. Well, nothing for me. What I want is for you to tell Camille who you are. No one else has to know if you don't want them to."

"What makes you think she would want to see me? I left her on the steps of a church!"

I shrugged. "Call it a hunch. A mother's intuition."

"I'll think about it."

Standing, I went to the door. Before opening it, I turned back to face her. "You're a courageous woman, Beverly. I hope you find it in yourself to go see your daughter before she leaves the hospital."

"You won't tell her?"

"It's not my story to tell." I'd done all I could do. The rest was up to Beverly.

***

Entering Camille's hospital room, I stopped in my tracks. "Oh. I didn't know you had company. I can come back later."

"No." Camille's voice was strong and somewhat pleading. "Please stay?"

Taking a few steps into the small private room, I set the vase of pink roses I'd brought on the windowsill. Nodding politely at the other woman standing next to Camille's bed, I stammered, "I just came to see for myself that you're going to be okay. I won't keep you."

"Violet. I think you know Beverly Carson."

144

The other woman held out her hand. "Violet. It's good to see you. I understand you're responsible for saving Camille's life." Reminding myself that Beverly's story wasn't mine to tell, I took her hand in mine and kept my own counsel.

I shrugged off the hero status. "I was just in the right or the wrong place at the right time."

"She's lucky she's alive. Detective Donaldson told me how she confronted the Everetts on the trail and nearly took a bullet in the process. If she hadn't met up with them on the trail when she did, the doctors say I would have bled out before anyone found me."

"What were you doing up there, anyway?" I asked.

Camille's expression instantly dimmed. "I'd just gotten home from the reading of Ned's will and wanted to see the land that cost him his life. I only planned to stay a few minutes, then those two showed up, and we argued. I tried to tell them that their concerns were moot. The only thing Ned left to me was some of his mother's jewelry. But Natalie was convinced I was going to inherit at least half of the Haggerty estate."

"Which was so wrong," Beverly chimed in. "I'm bound by the same attorney-client confidentiality as my boss. It killed me, pardon the pun, to keep my mouth shut, but I did. Maybe if I'd said something, Ned would still be alive."

"Keep your mouth shut about what?" I asked.

Camille shifted to sit up straighter. The effort clearly pained her, but once she was settled again, she filled me in. "Ned left all his land holdings in a trust for the county parks department with stipulations that nothing can be built on them other than hiking trails and buildings dedicated to education about the land and the wildlife that live there."

"So," Beverly added, "by killing Ned, the Everetts insured the land would never be sold or developed. They would have been better off trying to convince Ned to change his mind while he was alive."

"Wow." I let that information sink in. "Talk about ironic."

"I know, right?" Camille grimaced as she reached for the pink plastic cup with a straw protruding from the top. I was quicker and handed it to her. "Thanks." She took a sip and, closing her eyes, held the cup close for a moment. Opening her eyes, she took another sip, then indicated I should put it back on the table.

"What about the Renaissance Faire? Will it have to go?"

Beverly shook her head. "No. Ned stipulated their lease would remain unchanged for the next 100 years. After that, if the Faire still exists, it can be renewed in ten-year increments in perpetuity."

"And you knew this all along, but kept it to yourself?"

"I typed up Ned's will, and the codicil he added a few weeks ago when he found out about Camille."

"That's a lot to have on your shoulders," I said. "I don't think I could have kept from saying something."

"I wish I had said something, even if it cost me my job, but it's too late now. What's done is done."

Camille touched Beverly on the arm. "Ned wouldn't have blamed you either way. Besides, if you take that blame on yourself, then your boss does too. He knew what was in Ned's will. But then, who would have thought people would resort to murder over a zoning ordinance?"

We all let that sink in for a moment. "Not me, that's for sure," Beverly offered. "Hey, I need to go. I told my boss I'd only be gone a few minutes."

"Thanks for stopping by."

"If I can do anything for you, just let me know."

"I will. I promise."

When we were alone, I said, "She seems nice."

"I know. She feels awful about what happened, but it's not her fault. Some people let greed outweigh common sense, and Ned paid the price for it."

"And you, too. You could have died."

"But I didn't. My only regret is that I didn't have more time to get to know Ned. He had his peculiarities, but overall, he was a good man."

"I think you're right. Speaking of peculiarities, do you think Natalie is really pregnant? And, if she is, is the baby Ned's?"

"Detective Donaldson told me she's not pregnant. However, she *thinks* she is. Her attorney thinks a psychological examination will determine she's unfit to stand trial." She shook her head. "Then there's Paul. His defense is, "She told me to do it." That won't stand up in court."

"I don't suppose it will." It was time to change the subject. "So, when do you get out of here, and what's next for you?"

"My doctor said I can go home in a few days. Earl left today

in the old truck. He'll be back tomorrow with our car, so I don't
have to ride home in that rust bucket he bought."

"Ouch! Just thinking about riding in that thing again makes
my bones ache!"

"You and me both." Camille laughed, but cut herself off as the
movement aggravated her injury. When she composed herself, she
asked, "What about you?"

"Oh, I don't know. I think I'm just going to head out and see
where the wind blows me."

"Well, if it ever blows you in my direction, I hope you stop for
a visit."

"I'd love to."

CHAPTER THIRTY-TWO

Standing beside the open door of my truck, I willed the tears welling in my eyes to go away. My new friends, sans Millie, who'd gone on ahead to the vineyard where we would meet up, were all there. "I guess this is goodbye," I said. Bud, who sat behind the wheel, rested his head on my shoulder. I still wasn't a fan of dog slobber, but I'd become somewhat resigned to it. My canine companion had grown on me, and I couldn't imagine life on the road without him now.

"Ah, now, don't go getting all weepy-eyed on us," Bea guffawed. "We'll see you again, won't we, girls?"

"Absolutely," the group chorused.

Sherry stepped forward, wrapping me in a big hug. "I'll email you the details about the fall leaf-peeping route I plan to take. Maybe we can all meet up in New England?"

"Please do." New England in the fall hadn't been on our list, but only because Mason said he'd need to be back at work before then. We'd hoped to carve out a weekend to make the trip anyway. Now, I had nothing on my calendar. I could go wherever the wind blew me. "I've always wanted to see the fall colors."

"Me, too," Bea said. "Send me that itinerary, too. What about you, Kendra?"

"I'd love to, but I need to check my calendar. What days were you thinking?"

A lively discussion ensued, and soon, it was past time for me to go. "I hate to break this up, but I really need to get on the road."

"Of course you do!" Bea swallowed me in a hug. "And here we are, gabbing away." She shooed me into the truck and shut the door for me. Bud vaulted over the center console. He loved riding shotgun, especially if the window was down so he could stick his head out. Summer was still hanging on, so I cranked the engine and adjusted the air vents so Bud wasn't getting all the cool air. Putting the truck in gear, I checked my mirrors and, convinced that all was clear, I smiled and waved as I slowly pulled forward. I hadn't gone ten feet when a familiar nondescript sedan cut off my departure. "What the…?"

Detective Donaldson exited the car, carrying a brown paper bag with the word "Evidence" stamped across it. I rolled down my window as he approached.

"I'm glad I caught you before you left."

"I almost hit you!" My annoyance was real. I couldn't wait to see this town in my rearview mirror. Running him over would have kept me there indefinitely.

He smiled. It took me a moment to drag my gaze off his dimples and lovely orthodontia to the bag he held aloft. "You forgot to come by the station to pick up the things we took from your trailer."

"How did you know that wasn't going to be my first stop?"

"Was it?"

"No." I had wanted my coffee mug back but was willing to sacrifice it in the name of getting out of town.

Ray smirked as he thrust the bag at me. "I didn't think so. Everything is there." He stuck his head through the open window. "Hey, Bud. How's it hanging?" I rolled the back window down. Bud bounded into the back seat, anticipating a head rub. He wasn't disappointed.

While Bud got what he wanted, I opened the bag and peered inside. Besides the mug, I found a steak knife I hadn't realized was missing and a baggy with several strands of hair inside. I held it up. Ray explained. "It didn't match the hair we found on Ned's body."

"Oh." I stuffed it back in the bag and pulled out the smiley face mug. It appeared unharmed—a miracle, given its age and what I assumed was less-than-careful handling while in police custody. I put it back in the bag, rolled the top down, and stuffed the whole thing into the center console. I'd unpack it when I got to my next campsite.

"Hey." Ray continued to rub Bud's ears, but his attention was on me. "I thought you'd want to know. I asked Harvey Dreyer why he was so adamant that you had killed Ned."

I felt as if someone was stroking my ears. "What did he say?"

"He said he thought his son had done it, and right or wrong, he was trying to protect him."

"Seriously?"

Ray nodded. "Seriously. He knows what he did was wrong, and he handed his resignation to the mayor a few minutes ago. That's why I was late getting here."

I raised an eyebrow, silently asking for more details.

"The mayor has named me to be the interim chief of police."

I smiled. "Congratulations, Chief Donaldson." I was genuinely happy for him.

"I'm the interim chief, Mrs. Hartwell. Interim being the keyword."

"Do you want the job?"

"Hell, yes!"

"Then you'll get it." I put the truck in gear. "Now, Chief, if you'll move your car, I've got places to be and people to see."

He flashed his dimples again as he strutted back to his vehicle.

"You should give him a chance, Vi."

"Shut up, Mason."

Donaldson gave me a silent police escort to the edge of town, where he pulled off the road, and stood beside his car to wave goodbye as I passed. Bud barked his goodbye out the window. I flashed my headlights. It wasn't long before there was nothing but open road ahead of us. I shut off the air conditioner and powered the windows down.

"You feel that, Bud?" With his head out the window, he thumped his tail on the seat back in answer. "That's the wind at our backs. What do you say? Should we see where it takes us?"

ABOUT THE AUTHOR

As a young student living in the suburbs of Dallas at the time of the Kennedy assassination, D.W. Maroney grew up on a steady diet of conspiracy theories. To this day, D.W. still loves a good mystery and believes the truth of any event lies somewhere between the eyewitness accounts and the historical retelling. D.W. admits to being the only student who paid attention when the school librarian explained the use of the card catalog and other research materials. Where others saw only tedium, D.W. saw clues that would lead to fascinating facts hidden within the tomes and periodicals lining the shelves. During downtime, D.W. enjoys sorting through piles of musty old papers, scouring the depths of the internet, and looking for the one thing everyone else has overlooked.

D.W Maroney is a *USA Today* Best-selling author of genre fiction under the pseudonym Roz Lee.

Don't miss Violet's next adventure. Subscribe to D.W.'s newsletter today - https://mailchi.mp/866a03b74990/dw-maroney

See Violet's ever-growing collection of camp recipes on D.W.'s website – www.DWMaroney.com